Wataru Watari
Illustration **Ponkan⑧**

10.5

Contents

MY YOUTH R♥MANTIC C☻MEDY iS WRØNG, AS I EXPECTED

Wataru Watari

Illustration **Ponkan⑧**

VOLUME
10.5

YEN ON
NEW YORK

MY YOUTH ROMANTIC COMEDY IS WRONG, AS I EXPECTED Vol. 10.5
WATARU WATARI
Illustration by Ponkan⑧

Translation by Jennifer Ward
Cover art by Ponkan⑧

YAHARI ORE NO SEISHUN LOVE COME WA MACHIGATTEIRU.
Vol. 10.5 by Wataru WATARI
© 2011 Wataru WATARI
Illustration by PONKAN⑧
All rights reserved.
Original Japanese edition published by SHOGAKUKAN.
English translation rights in the United States of America, Canada, the United Kingdom, Ireland, Australia and New Zealand arranged with SHOGAKUKAN through Tuttle-Mori Agency, Inc.

English translation © 2021 by Yen Press, LLC

Yen On
150 West 30th Street, 19th Floor
New York, NY 10001

Visit us at yenpress.com
facebook.com/yenpress
twitter.com/yenpress
yenpress.tumblr.com
instagram.com/yenpress

First Yen On Edition: January 2021

Yen On is an imprint of Yen Press, LLC.
The Yen On name and logo are trademarks of Yen Press, LLC.

Library of Congress Cataloging-in-Publication Data
Names: Watari, Wataru, author. | Ponkan 8, illustrator.
Title: My youth romantic comedy is wrong, as I expected / Wataru Watari ; illustration by Ponkan 8.
Other titles: Yahari ore no seishun love come wa machigatteiru. English
Description: New York : Yen On, 2016–
Identifiers: LCCN 2016005816 | ISBN 9780316312295 (v. 1 : pbk.) | ISBN 9780316396011 (v. 2 : pbk.) |
    ISBN 9780316318068 (v. 3 : pbk.) | ISBN 9780316318075 (v. 4 : pbk.) | ISBN 9780316318082 (v. 5 : pbk.) |
    ISBN 9780316411868 (v. 6 : pbk.) | ISBN 9781975384166 (v. 6.5 : pbk.) | ISBN 9781975384128 (v. 7 : pbk.) |
    ISBN 9781975384159 (v. 7.5 : pbk.) | ISBN 9781975384135 (v. 8 : pbk.) | ISBN 9781975384142 (v. 9 : pbk.) |
    ISBN 9781975384111 (v. 10 : pbk.) | ISBN 9781975384173 (v. 10.5 : pbk.)
Subjects: | CYAC: Optimism—Fiction. | School—Fiction.
Classification: LCC PZ7.1.W396 My 2016 | DDC [Fic]—dc23
LC record available at http://lccn.loc.gov/2016005816

ISBNs: 978-1-9753-8417-3 (paperback)
        978-1-9753-8589-7 (ebook)

10 9 8 7 6 5 4 3 2 1

LSC-C

Printed in the United States of America

MY YOUTH R♥MANTIC C♥MEDY iS WR∅NG, AS I EXPECTED

ten and a half

Cast of Characters

Hachiman Hikigaya.......... The main character. High school second-year. Twisted personality.

Yukino Yukinoshita.......... Captain of the Service Club. Perfectionist.

Yui Yuigahama................. Hachiman's classmate. Tends to worry about what other people think.

Saika Totsuka................... In tennis club. Very cute. A boy, though.

Hayato Hayama................. Hachiman's classmate. Popular. In the soccer club.

Kakeru Tobe.................... Hachiman's classmate. An excitable character and member of Hayama's clique.

Iroha Isshiki.................... Manager of the soccer club. First-year student who was elected student council president.

Shizuka Hiratsuka............. Japanese teacher. Guidance counselor.

Komachi Hikigaya............. Hachiman's little sister. In her third year in middle school.

One of these days, we'll probably find a simple job even Yoshiteru Zaimokuza can handle.

As everyone on this planet knows, winters in Chiba don't mean much snow, but that doesn't necessarily mean it's not cold. Obviously, winters get chilly. In fact, I think it might get colder than some random snowy countries.

Most importantly, I've never spent time away from Chiba from late January to February, so I can't say for sure.

The only real point of comparison is the number on the thermometer, but even when the weather report announces it's below freezing, it's hard to tell exactly how cold it is without experiencing it.

So it could be true that the numbers on the thermometer don't translate to how cold it is in Chiba.

There's this term called *apparent temperature.*

Only through experience, perception, and education do you get a real feeling of what it is for the first time.

So if we take the above example…there was some dissonance between the numbers on the thermometer hanging on the wall of the clubroom and how it currently felt to me.

The main reason was the boy sitting in front of me.

Even though we were smack-dab in the middle of winter, he was sweating profusely, his mouth twisted up as he mopped his forehead with the back of one fingerless glove.

"…Mgh," he muttered solemnly. Yoshiteru Zaimokuza let his head hang.

In this posture, his neck was completely buried in his favorite trench coat, making him almost look like an avant-garde monument. Just the kind of thing installed at the entrance to a high-rise apartment building around Musashi-Kosugi with pretensions of being upper crust.

Zaimokuza refused to elaborate on that particular utterance, and the Service Club room was once again filled with silence.

There were supposedly others occupying the room besides myself and Zaimokuza, but they were either holding a cup of black tea and reading a book, deliberately oblivious to everything; scarfing down snacks and doing who-knows-what on their phone; or studying a compact mirror and finger-combing their bangs.

"…Mnghh," Zaimokuza groaned once more and looked up at the ceiling. This time, a greater sense of despair filled his voice. Still, nobody responded.

Though no one made as much as a stir, Zaimokuza continued to moan—over and over.

When the others finally reached their breaking point, I heard a little sigh come from the table diagonal to mine.

I peeked over at the captain of the Service Club, Yukino Yukinoshita, who set her teacup down on her saucer and pressed her temple. She flicked her gaze toward Zaimokuza, then straight at me. "…Maybe we should ask what he has to say?"

"Do we have to…? But even if we do ask, Snowflake is only gonna talk to Hikki," Yui Yuigahama replied lazily as she crunched on a rice cracker. Flopping over the desk, she rolled her head toward me.

Even though it took them some time to acknowledge Zaimokuza's presence, I thought they were being pretty nice to someone who'd just barged into the room.

The problem here was Iroha Isshiki, who was straight-up ignoring Zaimokuza as she made faces at her mirror. And why was she even here? *Well, whatever. I won't ask.*

Without even a glance in his direction, she finished checking her bangs, pulled some hand cream out of her pouch and then, humming, began to moisturize her hands. Her slim fingers slowly worked the cream into her skin, introducing a citrusy scent to the air around us.

Oh yeah, Isshiki and Zaimokuza don't know each other, huh? From her behavior, it was hard to believe she'd speak with Zaimokuza, even if they had been acquainted. Of course, the same could be said for the reverse.

So then..., I was thinking when Yuigahama interjected from her desk without sitting up.

"Why don't you ask him, Hikki?"

Her remark prompted a nod from Yukinoshita, as if that was obvious. "...You're right. This is Hikigaya's responsibility, after all."

"Don't foist this on me..."

I was only liable for Totsuka—down to the tiniest details. Call me "Tiny Tots" for short. Everyone knew I was a hard-core Totsuka stan. If he had concerts, I'd bring a homemade fan with his name on it. You know, "Tiny Tots" is kinda cute.

Anyway, I was the only one in this clubroom who could communicate with Zaimokuza. Though my gut told me this was going to be a hassle, I knew he was never going to leave if I didn't speak to him.

Steeling myself, I said, "Why are you here, Zaimokuza...?"

His head jerked up, and he smiled at me with some visible relief. "Oh-ho, if it isn't Hachiman! What a coincidence!"

"Can we skip the theatrics, please...?"

"Hapumf, so be it. Well, I've found myself in something of a conundrum…" He paused there. He adjusted his posture in his seat, gathering himself, and I automatically straightened up, too. "Have we already discussed the fact that I've been considering becoming an editor?"

"Nope. This is news to me." *There he goes, spewing his nonsense again…*, I thought.

Yuigahama, sitting to the side, muttered, "I thought you wanted to be a light something-or-other…?"

She was so generous to actually humor to him. The other two were largely ignoring him. Though Yukinoshita had paid attention to him for a moment, she was back to flipping a page in her paperback with a cool expression, deeming the conversation one not worth listening to. Isshiki had never given a damn at all, wearing a look of mild disgust as she mushed her lashes with an eyelash curler.

Yuigahama's objection was right. I'd thought Zaimokuza's dream was to be a light-novel author. At one point, he'd said he would be a game writer, but he'd immediately switched back to his original goal. His constant flip-flopping suggested to me that he might be best suited for a career in politics.

Anyway, when I glanced at Zaimokuza to question his change of heart, I saw him with arms folded, his expression solemn.

"Herm, well, a light-novel author is the bottom feeder of the entertainment world. 'Tis a job one can begin with nothing at all. Anyone can do it. Frankly, no one is jealous of those with this career, and the words *light novel* alone will have you treated like garbage…" His expression was leaden at first, but then his eyes flared wide. "…So I had a realization."

"Wh-what…?" Though I could sense something unpleasant behind the glint of his glasses, I couldn't stop myself from asking.

With a loud scrape of his chair, he got to his feet. "If you write, you'll just get canceled eventually! Take a break, and you'll disappear into oblivion! A rock by the side of the road in the industry! Is there any value in doing this job?!"

His voice pealed through the clubroom, ringing in my head. When the echo subsided, he sat himself down again, and a tranquil atmosphere settled over us once more.

Despite his volume, he received the same cold reception. I realized even Yuigahama, who had been kindly listening to him, was now scrolling on her phone.

Now, the only one listening to him talk was me. I was used to being alone, but this feeling of isolation stung.

"U-uh-huh…you know a lot about this…," I said without much thought, not knowing how to respond. It was hard to comment on.

Zaimokuza smirked. "I saw it online."

Wow. The World Wide Web sure was something. You could find just about anything on there.

That little exchange was enough for me to be quite done with this conversation, but Zaimokuza's opining yet continued. "But in that realm, an editor is admired! Not only have they a stable career, 'tis a creative job—one that might even be close to working at an animation studio! Which means I might be able to marry a voice actress! Fwa-ha-ha-ha-ha!"

"Someone get this guy a Happy Meal. Do they make a Slaphappy Meal…?"

He was happier than if Christmas, New Year's, and his birthday came on the same day. Maybe even Halloween and Valentine's Day. Totally unrelated, but why do we wish other people "Happy Halloween" and "Happy Valentine's Day" in English? What was there to be so happy about? I mean, Valentine's Day is the anniversary of Saint Valentine's death… Who knows? Maybe it won't be long until we start wishing each other "Happy April Fool's Day," too.

Zaimokuza was basically the personification of the modern trend of tacking *happy* onto every holiday—like, that was crazy! How is it crazy, you ask? It just was.

For starters, his end goal of marrying a voice actress was already crazy.

Marriage rates were already on the decline! A random light-novel author had no chance of marrying a voice actress! Forget it!

I didn't really give a damn if Zaimokuza refused to get his head out of the clouds and ended up wasting the rest of his life, but I just had to make sure to educate him on one thing. This was just an act of kindness from a classmate.

"Zaimokuza."

"Wh-what…?"

Zaimokuza sat up in his seat and looked me dead in the eye—maybe because I had unconsciously pitched my voice lower or let myself sound more forceful.

I spoke slowly. "When you were a middle schooler, did you ever think you'd automatically find a girlfriend once you were in high school?"

"Ngh!" I must have hit the nail on the head. He said nothing, greasy sweat beading on his forehead.

I followed up with another blow. "And I bet you're thinking you'll automatically find a girlfriend once you're in college now!"

"Nghhhhh! H-how did you know…?!"

He didn't even need to ask. The answer was obvious.

"Because everyone follows the same path…" My voice cracked from emotion.

There was once a time when I'd thought that, too. When you're a wee little kid, you just don't know your place—you're ignorant to the ways of the world. You think you'll be married with kids at twenty-five. As you go through middle and high school, you start to get a better grip on society, and you begin to lower your standards so they're more realistic. In a world like ours, where you can't even have little dreams…

As I was mulling over these matters, a cold, dry chuckle slipped out of me. In a moment of synchrony, Zaimokuza blew a heavy, ice-cold sigh.

I heard someone quietly clear their throat before making a peep. "Everyone, huh? ...I see."

"Hmm..."

When I looked over, Yukinoshita was peeking at me, no longer focused on the book she had been reading. When our eyes met, she quickly turned away. Meanwhile, Yuigahama had her fingers hovering over her phone, her expression frozen in a strained look.

And then the clubroom went silent.

Huh? Why's it all quiet...?

The uncomfortable vibe was making me fidget. Isshiki looked up from her compact mirror to glance over at us before letting out a short sigh. "...Not like I care, but is it easy to get into a publishing firm?"

She'd been totally ignoring us, so I was certain she hadn't been listening, but apparently, she'd heard our conversation.

That remark defrosted the air. Though Isshiki hadn't directed her question at anyone in particular, Yukinoshita cocked her head in response. "I think I recall hearing publishing houses have a high barrier for entry..."

"Ohhh, okay. Sounds tough." From the way Yuigahama replied, it was fairly dubious if she got this.

Does she even understand what sort of work a publishing house does...?

Leaving Yuigahama aside for the moment, what Yukinoshita was saying was true. I also remembered hearing from my dad that getting into the media industry wasn't easy. *All right, what does Zaimokuza think about taking up this challenge...?* I wondered, returning my attention to him and finding him surprisingly composed.

"Aye. I have also researched online, and they say 'tis an arduous trial." Zaimokuza folded his arms and tilted his head, groaning. "But how inscrutable… Just what's so difficult about it…? Editing a light novel is so simple, one could do it while asleep. It's a simple job anyone can do. You just need to read the finished drafts. Or send an e-mail to whoever's ranked at the top on Let's Do a Novelist and offer them a publishing deal, right?"

"Uh… Uh-huh…"

Hard to believe he'd once aspired to be a light-novel author himself. Well, no one really knows what these authors do, so maybe this sort of misunderstanding was inevitable.

Obviously, being a light-novel editor had to be hard work. I mean, just having to deal with dumbass authors like Zaimokuza alone would be enough to give you nausea, heartburn, indigestion, upset stomach, diarrhea? Pepto-Bismol! I bet bad light-novel authors made the editors shoulder the blame for their mistakes.

"Well, you won't know until you try getting hired," I said.

"Tsk, tsk, tsk." Zaimokuza clicked his tongue as he waved his finger. He was so obnoxious… "I have, of course, come up with a plan to get employed."

"Oh…? I'm listening."

"'Tis true that it's difficult to get hired straight out of university. But changing jobs is another matter! When you're on *my* level, you can slip into an editing agency or smaller publisher and get hired at a better company after you have sufficient experience," Zaimokuza said with the utmost arrogance, a cocky smile on his face as he leaned back, chuckling to himself.

Mysteriously enough, his confidence almost made me believe him.

"Ohhh, you've actually considered this…" Yuigahama, meanwhile, just fell for it hook, line, and sinker.

"Uh, but how do you manage to complete step one…?" I said. He certainly had a picture of a career plan—a picture that essentially amounted to a poorly drawn cartoon.

It seemed Yukinoshita also realized this fact instantly, as her eyebrows came together in a serious look. "I believe smaller publishers don't actively recruit…"

However, Zaimokuza's eardrums refused to let in anything that didn't align with his agenda. "And so it struck me: If I could get editing experience while I'm a student, then I could get insta-hired at Gagaga Bunko, at least…"

"Have a little more respect for Gagaga…"

Say what you will, Shogakukan was still one of the Big Three… The way he determinedly shrugged off reality was almost a fresh take, but that was beside the point.

The issue was his statement after that.

"And I was thinking, in order to build editing experience, how about trying to compose a *doujinshi*?"

"Huhhh. Well, good luck," I said.

"Aye… However, I lack *a true partner* who would make a *doujinshi* with me… A *true partner* who could see and hear the same things as I…"

"Uh… Uh-huh…"

That phrase was giving me the chills… *Why is he repeating it? I have a bad feeling about this…*

As I was shaking, Zaimokuza clapped a hand on my shoulder as if to stop my trembling.

He flashed me a smile so bright, it could practically illuminate the whole world. "So I was thinking…Hachiman, let's make one together!"

"No. And we're not friends."

You couldn't illuminate my world with *that* kind of enthusiasm! He might as well have been calling out to me, like, *Isono, let's play ball!* I was permanently banishing myself from this party. I might be inclined to help him out if he was willing to pay me to stay.

"Hachimaaaan! I thought we were friends forever! Why are you so mean?!" Zaimokuza wailed. "Meanie, meanie!"

There was no way I was going to babysit Zaimokuza. As I was ignoring his whining, I heard a compact mirror snapping shut.

I looked over to see Isshiki, who had finished with her little grooming routine—or fixing herself or whatever—and was now tucking her mirror away in her pouch. Then she stuck up her index finger, put it against her chin, and tilted her head contemplatively. "Ummm, what's a *doujinshi*?"

"Well," I explained, "basically, it's a self-published book. You draw a manga or whatnot yourself, and make a book out of it."

"…Huhhh." I could almost see the question mark floating above Isshiki's head. I was no expert, so I didn't really know how to get it across to her.

While I was searching for another way to explain, Yuigahama shot up her hand, looking like she wanted someone to call on her.

"I know about the thing—Comiket, right? You draw manga yourself. I think Hina was talking about it recently."

"You barely understand it at all, and Ebina's hobbies are…a little unique, but, well, you got the gist of it," I said.

This time, Yukinoshita was the one to tilt her head, looking unconvinced. "It doesn't have to be manga. Personally, my impression of it leans more in the literary direction."

"Oh yeah, there's that, too."

If you traced it back to its roots, I was pretty sure it was something done by literary giants and big-time authors. Things like *Shirakaba* and *Garakuta Bunko* were in textbooks.

It was true that *doujinshi* covered a wide range of publications—not only manga, but essays and meta on various subjects, or photo collections. Even within each genre, you could find a whole range of content.

"Meta-analysis" is a simple term, but it could cover everything from a critique of military affairs to a general review of the past anime season, or even on how to win a game of rock-paper-scissors that followed a

Sunday anime. In the broader classification of *doujinshi*, there could be cosplay, animation, music, drama CDs made by independent creators, and character merch—everything but the kitchen sink.

After I carefully selected examples for my summary, Isshiki nodded. "Ohhh, Comiket, huh…? I've heard of it before."

Did you know, Raiden? Well, the event was picked up for TV specials, so it wasn't unusual.

However, it seemed Isshiki's knowledge on the subject was somewhat biased. "You can make a boatload of money, right?" she asked as she leaned forward, deep interest in her sparkling, puppy-dog eyes.

Though her body language was that of a pure, innocent, and chaste maiden, what she was saying was the worst…

"Uh, not necessarily. I'm told they're not doing it for the money."

For starters, the assumption is that creators make them for content, not for profit. Not that I would know. I've heard these groups break even at best—and after expenses, they're usually in the red.

"…You do it…even when it doesn't make you money?" Isshiki said, then groaned, taking her head in her hands. She was really struggling to make sense of this…

"It means this falls in the realm of hobbies." Yukinoshita nodded firmly.

Well, it seems like she throws down a fair amount of money on her hobbies, like tea or Ginnie the Grue or cat merch or whatever, so maybe that sort of thing actually sits well with her.

"It's kind of amazing, though."

The way Yuigahama was munching on her snacks, she didn't seem especially impressed, but maybe she was in her own way. She offered some oohs and aahs regardless.

"It isn't really all that uncommon," I said. "I mean, wanting to make a book isn't reserved for geeks."

"*Really?*" Isshiki replied, sounding rather doubtful.

It seemed she still wasn't convinced. It wasn't surprising she should feel that way, since this was so distant from her own life.

But if we were going with similar examples, there were others. "There's the free magazines that university students often make, right? Look, it's like that," I said.

Yuigahama clapped her hands. "The things they hand out at school festivals."

"…Ohhh, I know that." Isshiki nodded, apparently following us.

"Right? In other words, a free magazine is *doujinshi* for your pretentious types."

"It sounds a lot cruder when you put it like that, but that description is oddly fitting…" Yukinoshita seemed to be remembering something unpleasant, fingers pressed against her temple.

What a coincidence. I started dissociating while I was saying it.

"But regardless," I said, "though I may have inspired some bias regarding free magazines, I believe we've managed to attain a definite alignment on this matter. Of course, discussion of a free magazine necessitates operating on a case-by-case basis, so in light of that fact, in order to reach actionable agreeance, moving forward, as thought leaders, we have no choice but to commit to results through repeat iteration."

"What are you talking about…?" Isshiki was weirded out. It looked as if her chair had retreated a few centimeters.

"Ah, sorry. I got a little self-conscious for a moment there…"

"*Un*conscious would have been preferable…" Yukinoshita sighed in exasperation.

Anyway, these two activities had something in common: They were both hobbies. Not much distinguishes creators of free magazines from *doujinshi* circles. In other words, they are a subgenre of *otaku* known as the "pretentious type."

To put it another way: There are as many *doujinshi* out there as there are genres, as there are people.

"So what kind of book are you planning to make?" I asked Zaimokuza.

He lost himself in deep thought for a while, and when he looked up again, his eyes were piercing. "Herm. I thought perhaps a novel after all... Since I'm not particularly knowledgeable about anything, and I can't draw."

Yikes, that rationale was just pathetic.

Could we please put an end to the trope of a bad artist becoming a light-novel author? I wish people would at least go for it based on a legitimate reason, like the fact that they can't get a real job.

"So it all comes back to light novels, huh...?" I said. "If you want to write one, then you can advertise it on the Internet. Like on that site you mentioned earlier, Let's Do a Novelist. In fact, wouldn't you have higher chances of making your big break there?"

Huh, that's weird—I had given Zaimokuza some actual constructive criticism.

But his reaction was lacking enthusiasm. "Herm... I have no fondness for such things."

"Why not? It's a good idea. And the *isekai* reincarnation OP harem thing is really hot right now."

"...What?" Isshiki made a low noise like *What the heck is he talking about...?*

What's with that look? ...Did I just say something weird?

It seemed I had after all.

Chairs scraped as the girls gathered their seats together for a hushed conference.

"I...seka? O—what? What did he just say...?" Yukinoshita pondered.

"What's…opie harem?"

"Isn't that, like, a brand of gummy bears?"

Going old school there, Isshiki.

An *isekai* reincarnation OP harem story is where the protagonist is reborn in another world with some power that makes him invincible, and builds a gang of girls. Crap, explaining it makes it sound more absurd.

Well, as long the people who like that stuff are reading it. Don't like it? Don't read it. It's not exactly begging for mainstream acceptance.

With *isekai* OP reincarnation stories—and light novels, and all that sort of thing to begin with—they just have to please their fans.

Well, this isn't limited to light novels.

It's true with anything. With words, or with feelings.

It's enough if it reaches the person you want to make happy or communicate to.

However, for some reason, this was not at all getting through to Mr. Zaimokuza.

He was continuing to ignore our conversation, flailing around his arms and legs as he desperately tried to make his appeal. "Nuooo! This is about nothing of the sort! It's not about popularity or sales or *anything* like that! I care naught for such things!! It's just, uh, well… You know! I just loathe being forced into the framework of a ranking or a list! I simply do not wish my works to be judged before they're displayed!"

For a second there, I'd gotten deluded into thinking he was saying something cool, but the word choices caught my attention. And from that arose but one answer.

"Oooh. Stories get ranked on that site, huh? Well, I guess it's a little tough to face the unpopularity of your work."

"Nay! Nay, I say! I am not in the least concerned with ranking or placing or numbers or reviews! Rankings are naught but a rough yardstick! The rest, one makes up for with courage!" Zaimokuza raved with enthusiastic zeal.

But some deficiencies can't be supplemented with courage alone. It was beyond transparent what he was worried about here—*I can see right through you!*

"…Ohhh. So you actually did post, and it broke your spirit."

"That's quite some progress," said Yukinoshita. "You would have to steel yourself to place that in public."

"Yeah, yeah, that's courageous!" Yuigahama added.

Both of them complimented him like they were half-surprised and half-impressed. At least, I think they were complimenting him. Right? Whew! And here I thought they were coming in with some sarcasm! Well, I guess it doesn't take much to detect it in Yukinoshita.

I felt like I could give the guy a compliment.

Even if it was just online, this guy who hadn't even been able to complete a manuscript before—never mind applying for a newcomer's award—had uploaded his work where it could be seen. It really warmed my heart to think that now there would be people aside from me who would read it and suffer. Everyone should suffer more. If everyone were to suffer, then surely we would have peace in the world.

Or so I thought, but Zaimokuza was waving his hands, like *Nah.* "No, I submitted not. The thought merely occurred to me after I saw other stories that got slammed."

"Oh, I see…"

It seems world peace is yet distant.

As expected of Zaimokuza. They don't call him a useless wannabe for nothing. Well, from another angle, you could say his ability to observe other people's work being trashed and sympathize with them to this degree meant he possessed a high level of empathy. Hmm, he might be more suited to being a writer than you'd think…

However, I personally believe the thing most necessary to write a light novel is not empathy. It's not even good prose. It's not even a grasp of story structure or a rich imagination.

I think what you need is mental fortitude.

You have to be someone who doesn't give in to other people's opinions, whose spirit won't break even when the books don't sell, who won't spill the tea on a blog or Twitter, who remains humble even if the books do well, who doesn't get discouraged even when derided by important people, who won't strike back over some drama, who won't be too focused by some random dumpster fire, who won't develop an ego, who never even believed in themselves in the first place, who doesn't worry about the future or retirement even though they constantly loom overhead, who might be in tears on a lonely night, who will never get their hopes up from good news, who doesn't compare themselves with other authors, who won't abandon their project just because they can't write anymore, who won't run away from an impending deadline, and who won't forget to be grateful to others.

These "16 No-Nos" were necessary to be a light-novel author.

Mental fortitude. That's the most important thing. I seem to recall that the author of the light novel *A Sister's All You Need* wrote something like that in a book. Maybe? Probably not.

But Zaimokuza wasn't a pro, and I knew full well that he had no guts, so I had to guide him in a direction that reduced hassle for me as much as possible! Zaimokuza's mental state was as fragile as tofu. I would recommend tossing it in a stew at this time of year.

I straightened myself in my seat and cleared my throat. I assumed a somewhat calmer tone than usual. "Zaimokuza, I don't think your *doujinshi* will sell a single copy. Isn't facing that reality painful enough on its own?"

It seemed he could imagine such a scenario vividly, as he choked up. Enduring the heat and cold in the summer and the winter as he patiently remained on standby alone at his table, hearing the voices of the popular cosplayers at the table beside him being friendly with each other, gazing at the people in the winding line for another booth on the other side, desperately staring into the air to avoid looking at his untouched stack of books… Would Zaimokuza be able to survive such a situation? Nay. Nay, I say.

Eventually, his shoulders slumped. "…You have a point," he rasped.

"If you're trying to be an editor, then don't make a *doujinshi*. It'd be more constructive to think up some other way," I said, verbally kicking him while he was down.

"Herm… I see…," Zaimokuza agreed meekly. It seemed I had successfully broken his spirit.

Nice. Now I won't be forced into making one with him…

Now that Zaimokuza had quieted his booming voice, the clubroom was suddenly still again.

I was sighing in relief, figuring we'd reached the end of that, when there came the crunch of a rice cracker. "But, like, how do you become an editor?" Yuigahama asked, munching away.

Zaimokuza's head jerked up with a gasp. "Aye, indeed…"

Now that she mentioned it, it made me a little curious, too. "Guess I'll give it a quick search…"

As Zaimokuza had said, everything was on the Internet. Including things I wished weren't there.

"Yukinoshita, let me use the laptop," I said.

"…This isn't a computer room," she grumbled, but she got up, pulled out the laptop, and briskly set it up for me.

Figuring I'd just start asking Professor Google, I sat down in front of the laptop. As I did, I heard a scrape as a chair was pulled up beside me.

Looking over, I found Yukinoshita sitting to my right, cheerfully pulling her glasses from her bag. She swept back her glossy black hair with a gentle hand, then slowly slid the glasses onto her face with the care of a coronation. Her thin, graceful fingertips slowly came away from the frames. Her eyelashes were so long that when she blinked, it looked as if they would just about touch the lenses. Once she was ready, she gave a little nod to no one in particular, then quietly scooted her chair closer to peer at the laptop.

Her hair swished, smelling of soap.

She's so close...

It made me so antsy for her to breach my personal space, I shifted my chair slightly to the left—whereupon the faint scent of citrusy perfume tickled my nose.

I hadn't even noticed Yuigahama circling around to my left side.

When she slumped forward to lean her chin on the desk, her elbow bumped into mine, and our glances flickered back and forth, silently offering the spot to each other. Right when I was thinking maybe she'd let me take the space, she looked away, refusing to budge an inch. So then I was getting ready to move, but I felt my blazer cuff rubbing against Yuigahama's skirt, and I couldn't do anything anymore.

...So close.

And then I sensed something behind me.

The rubber squeak of indoor shoes sounded on the floor.

Turning just my head, I saw Isshiki standing behind me. She popped her face over my shoulder, peering at the computer screen. She was leaning a bit of her body weight on me—the feel and heat of her small hand on my shoulder caught my attention. I could hear her shallow breathing, too. It made something like a shiver run down my spine.

...I said you're too close.

With both sides and behind me occupied, I had no choice but to lean forward.

But even the space before me was blocked.

Zaimokuza came over to hover right in front of me, his head

thrusting down from above like one of those bald, long-necked *youkai* as he looked down upon the laptop.

Too close. Back off.

Under this weird pressure from virtually every direction, I tried to make myself as small as possible and typed out the keywords that came to mind. Instantly, countless search results were displayed. "Job searching sites and message boards… Huh. There's a prep school for people seeking employment in publishing… All sorts of stuff…"

"Oh, Hikki! What about this?" As I was skimming over the items that seemed noteworthy, Yuigahama leaned forward to point at the screen.

Yukinoshita tilted her head toward me as well, reading aloud the item pointed out to me. "'A Success Story'… It seems like this is from the blog of someone who managed to get employed at a publishing house. That might be good."

"Go on, go on." Isshiki tapped on my shoulder, urging me along.

Seriously, you're too close. It's making my back all sweaty, so if you could please back up like six inches…

When I glanced at Zaimokuza in front of me to get his input, he gave me a big nod. "Aye, it seems a fine choice!"

"…All right, then let's take a look." Clicking on the link, I went to the home page of this so-called success story.

On the header in a big font was a title that read ***The Best or Bust! Kenken's Journal to Get That Top-Class Publishing Job Offer!***

"…Hey, what does *top-class job offer* mean?" I asked. "How do they decide the rankings for job offers?"

"Wait a moment," Yukinoshita said, suddenly reaching out from the side to open up a new tab and search for this "top offer" thing. As she did, her long black hair kept touching my hand and then moving away again, and it was ticklish. I reflexively drew my hand back and laid it on my lap politely.

Once the search results came up, her finger pointed to the screen. "It seems that, though it's not publicized, there is an internal ranking of candidates at companies. The highest on that list is the top offer. From the moment of their hire, that person is treated as a candidate for management and is at an advantage during assignments…according to this."

"Hmm…the words *candidate for management* alone make me uneasy…"

This sounded like a corrupt workplace. That phrase unsettled me as much as "we're like family here" or "a great place for young people to take the lead!" It made me concerned for the fate of Mr. Kenken.

All right, while we're sating our thirst for horror, let's trace this Mr. kenken guy's path of glory and see whether he did succeed in getting his top offer and became a corporate slave at a publishing company.

I decided to scroll on down the screen and read his entries in order.

The Best or Bust! Kenken's Journal to Get That Top-Class Publishing Job Offer!

On this blog, I will be chronicling events on my way to getting a good offer from a publishing company!

All rights reserved. ©kenken

1: Fill out an application form.

Or, in common parlance, a job app (lol).

Aside from the standard stuff like a summary, your work history, and the reason for your application, each company will have their unique prompts on this form, including an essay section, three subjects for an impromptu story the applicant must create, a news story that's recently caught your interest, three people you have your eye on right now, a story of your greatest embarrassment or a failure, etc.… Some sections may be a little odd, such as a

blank half page that says, "Please use this space freely to brag about yourself."

Sometimes the career center at your school will hold on to samples of old forms, so it also may be worth asking older students from your classes or clubs to show you theirs!

Regarding your resume...

These days, it's becoming more common on applications to not have to fill in the name of your university, so it's not necessarily the case that you will be at a disadvantage based on the prestige of your institution. In fact, I'm personally skeptical that such a bias exists at all—in fact, I believe the fact that many students who receive offers from major companies are from prestigious universities is not due to the power of the university brand, but perhaps just that people with the capacity to be selected attend prestigious universities.

It's my belief that moving forward, many companies will venture to evaluate candidates on a personal and individual basis, more equally and without bias.

And conversely, job hunters should also not judge companies by their brand or established reputation. The secret to success may be the awareness that just as we are chosen by the company, we are also in the position of choosing a company.

And I will offer you these words:

"When you gaze long into the abyss, the abyss also gazes into you."

—Nietzsche

Oh-ho... Just at a glance, it looks like he's saying some fairly legitimate stuff. But hey, I had to get that secondhand from kenken? I wish I could have heard it straight from Nietzsche instead!

Yukinoshita had been gazing at the screen along with me, *hmm*ing as she read along.

But Yuigahama and Isshiki were both looking *meh* and seemed a bit put off. "Too wordy…," Yuigahama muttered.

Hey, if that discourages you, you'll never be able to finish, Case Closed. *When you're hooked, you're hooked, no matter what the word count is!*

I felt an irritated tapping on my shoulder. "This guy gets on my nerves…," Isshiki said with unconcealed annoyance as her finger continued to tap my shoulder.

Uh-huh. Could you stop taking it out on me?

I could sympathize—this piece was weirdly aggravating.

Who knows why it was so snooty, but maybe a pretentious university student would talk this way. Thinking about those types makes me not want to go to university…

Anyway, this kenken guy sure was champing at the bit. If the rest of the entries were gonna be this enthusiastic, it'd make me lose the urge to keep reading. About the only people with this much energy have got to be the Kinki Kids, or Yoshida Terumi.

"Herm…I see. Let's read the next one, Hachiman!"

I was doubtful Zaimokuza actually understood this, but I nodded back at him and clicked on the next page.

2: The written exam.

Many companies will post general commonsense questions, but there is the rare occasion when a company will make you take the SPI. They sell books with example problems, so make sure to prepare for that beforehand. The SPI is essential for most businesses. Furthermore, even those transferring from a different job rather than applying straight from university will sometimes have to take the test, so there's no harm in being prepared. When it comes to the written exam, my personal feeling is that Shu——sha and Ko——sha set standard questions that probe examinees more broadly, while I get the impression Ka——wa Shoten's exam has

more trick questions designed to make you fail. Be very careful if you're taking the Ka——wa Shoten test!

This guy trying to play it cool while oozing resentment toward K-shoten… I could infer this kenken guy had failed that particular written exam.

"What's an SPI, Hachiman? A spy?" Zaimokuza's voice came down from above.

"Wasn't it some kinda magazine?" Yuigahama responded. "Maybe it's reading material, 'cause this is a publishing company?"

"You're talking about *SPA!*…"

What the heck is a *SPA!* exam? Do they have questions like "Name the top thirty best *gyoza* restaurants in Shinbashi"? But I feel like the written exam at a publishing company would give you questions like something from a TV show, so I can't necessarily deny it, scarily enough.

I didn't really know anything about this SPI exam myself. Given that I was at a loss as to how to reply, Yukinoshita quietly reached for the computer. Opening up yet another tab, she started to search for the SPI.

When she eventually found the page she was looking for, she stroked her chin and nodded.

"Simply put, the SPI refers to an aptitude test. It seems to be a sort of analysis of your overall profile by testing on logical thinking and mathematical and linguistic ability, as well as a personality test," Yukinoshita summarized as she pushed her glasses up with her middle finger.

Yuigahama's jaw was slack with confusion. "Huhhh… Oh, so it's kind of like those little flowchart tests in the magazines? I can get that!" she said brightly, cocking her head a bit as she turned toward Yukinoshita.

Yukinoshita's head turned the opposite way, as if resigning herself. "…Sure. I suppose that's close enough."

"No, it's really not," I objected.

"Please don't give up trying to explain, Yukinoshita...," Isshiki said.

That seemed to make Yukinoshita reconsider, and she closed her eyes and began to ponder the matter. "A-all right. If I come up with the right way to put it, it should get through to Yuigahama, shouldn't it? A way for Yuigahama to get it... A way for Yuigahama to get it...," Yukinoshita muttered quietly to herself as she considered with utmost earnestness.

Yuigahama watched her, shoulders slumping. "Y-your kindness kinda hurts, Yukinon..."

Well, explaining an exam you've never taken is bound to be hard, as would be understanding that explanation. This is something you'd have to experience for yourself to get. I was sure we'd understand once we started to eventually look for jobs—whether we liked it or not. Agh, I really didn't want to look for a job...

But, well, a written exam is something you can prepare for, so you could say that's on the better side.

The hard part of job hunting is the interview that comes after.

Now then, how did our kenken make it through this challenge? I decided to forge ahead. *Show me what you've got.*

3: The first interview.
Sometimes you'll have interviews as a group.
That guy from K—— University was constantly interrupting, and it annoyed the shit out of me. It's his fault I blew it. I hope he rots in hell.

That was the only thing written in the third entry. *Your explanations have suddenly gotten sloppy, huh, kenken? But then your complaints about this guy are the one thing you made sure to put in.*

There really wasn't much there, but Zaimokuza closely scrutinized the screen, looking over it a number of times. "Hooom? Is there naught else written here, Hachiman?"

"Looks like. I'm going to the next one."

There wasn't much to say with so little information.

I got the okay from the girls to proceed, then moved the mouse and clicked to the next page.

4: The second interview.

That guy from a certain F——sha who stirred shit up saying, "Oh, well *said*." I think he was probably editor-in-chief level. He can go to hell, too.

There was hardly any explanation here at all anymore. He was just venting.

As we read along through kenken's job-hunting journal, which quickly took a turn for the worse, a humorless laugh escaped me.

From beside me, I heard a sigh slip from Yukinoshita. "It seems there's less and less specific information here, hmm?"

"It's actually getting more specific, but in all the wrong ways..." Isshiki made a face, looking exasperated.

As the two said, the content was clearly thinning out. Maybe this kenken guy was getting a little discouraged at this point. I was getting a little discouraged reading it. Job hunting seems rough...

But we were only at the second interview. This journal still had more to go.

I stretched out to get ready, then moved on to the next entry in the journal.

5: The third interview.

A high-pressure interview. There were about ten higher-ups from Ko——sha all in a row. It was bad. Maybe even twenty. It was bad.

This wasn't even venting anymore. Kenken's initial spirit had evaporated, and he was already on his last legs. In fact, content aside, I could even compliment his mental fortitude in making the effort to actually write this out.

Since he'd expressly stated it was a high-pressure interview, it must have been tremendously stressful. Even in such a short entry, you could keenly sense the terror and despair.

Though this was something we could only imagine, an interview in front of the company executives seemed super-tough. A line of important older men with fancy titles like board member or executive or director in black suits—that's practically like Seele. That's beyond impact; that's Second Impact.

"That seems kinda brutal...," Yuigahama murmured, her voice filled with sympathy and sorrow. Even I was feeling a little bit pained right then.

"There's still more...," Yukinoshita said with some difficulty. Depending on how you took her tone, it could even come off like she was pushing us to stop looking at this now.

But since we'd come this far, I would see it to the end. No, I had a duty. With a trembling hand, I moved the cursor and clicked on the final entry.

6: The final interview.
To the assholes from mass-ken who lied and said the last interview is just to confirm your interest so you can't get dropped—you're full of shit. You do just get dropped.

The journal ended there.

Just what on earth had become of kenken? Thinking about his fate made my heart ache.

And it seemed I wasn't the only one. We were all breathing deep sighs.

I was sure it was partly out of guilt from having gotten a glimpse of a microcosm of one man's life, and the misery of being witness to the harshness at the front lines of a job hunt.

I think more than anything else, the greatest sentiment was that we really didn't want to work with a guy who would write a journal like this, either. I mean, he was all into it at first, but then for the latter half, it was mostly resentment and complaints...

"Um...but heeey, this guy wasn't accepted, right?" Isshiki said hesitantly.

Yuigahama seemed to have that sudden realization as well, and she did a double take at the screen. "...You're right! Even though it says it's a success story!"

"Ah, well, it's like... With this sort of thing, you just go ahead and write *success* when you start. It's like the law of attraction. A visualization exercise for pretentious types."

"I believe that's not quite visualization so much as a type of self-help, though...," Yukinoshita said, pressing her temple.

Yeah, but job hunting does have a sort of self-improvement element to it, right...? I mean, just from what we'd been seeing here with this net surfing, it was stacked with shiny new words like *self-analysis*, *self-promotion*, and *desire for growth*. I'm sure what businesses want is energetic, unbending, unyielding employees with mental stability, so maybe that's inevitable, but the way they're all trying to show off this same cheerful character is so unnatural, it's scary.

At any rate, there doesn't seem to be a field for me..., I was thinking, my desire-to-work meter plummeting, when Zaimokuza, standing in front of me, said quietly, "Hachiman, what's a mass-ken? Is it like Chiba-ken?"

"Uh, they're nothing alike. Come on, do you even know what Chiba-ken is when you say that?"

Chiba-ken is the mascot character of the Chiba Prefecture Environment Foundation, and its design is the shape of Chiba prefecture made into a dog. When I say that, you might think it's exactly the same as Chiiba-kun, but this is shockingly different. For something that has the "dog" kanji in its name, it's incredibly undoglike. In fact, Chiiba-kun, which claims to be a mysterious animal that just looks like a dog, is much more doglike. Seriously, what is the deal with Chiba's taste? This prefecture is really weird sometimes, man.

Yukinoshita tilted her head. "Well, I'm sure it's a nickname for a mass media research club."

"Research... Sounds like they'd do some real cool things, like experiments and stuff," Yuigahama muttered, gazing vacantly into space.

The word *research* was probably making her imagine all sorts of things. But I think Miss Gahama's impression of wearing white coats and waving flasks and beakers around might not be quite right!

But it's true enough that from just the term *research*, it's difficult to picture specifically what they do. If it were science and technology or history, then you could imagine something, even if only vaguely. But for research on mass media, I couldn't quite come up with anything.

"...While we're at this, how about we look up these mass-ken things," I suggested.

"Aye. Do as you must!" Zaimokuza emphatically agreed with a dramatic flutter of his coat like William Smith Clark, so I decided to immediately seek education from Professor Google. I typed in the name of some random university, hit Space, then added *mass-ken*.

And there they came pouring out: a parade of pretentious statements. There were self-introductions with photos of themselves in suits, personal mottos, and shameless plugs, and along with that, a ton of supportive comments from their friends.

On top of that, with their photos of everything from traveling in India and climbing Mount Fuji to BBQ at an employment seminar camp, I had no idea what it was they were researching.

It was unbearable to look at directly, so I squinted to skim over it and basically got the idea.

Essentially, this was a club where people who sought to get hired at TV stations, newspapers, and publishing companies would get together to exchange information and teach each other how to successfully get a job.

"H-hey, Hachiman. Do you need to get into one of these mass-ken things to get into a publisher? Definitely? Really?" Seeing the photos of people having fun posted on the home page, Zaimokuza started to panic.

"Well, I doubt it's absolutely necessary. In fact, based on what I'm seeing, I even get the feeling it would be better to not join…"

I'm sure many of these clubs that call themselves media research societies or advertisement research societies are actually doing that.

But when I hear that ring of pretention, I can't help but imagine the face of that Mr. Tamanawa, student council president of Kaihin High School, and it does not give me a good vibe.

What's more, looking at this site, I discovered a concerning line of text. "…I don't think you could get in with these guys anyway, Zaimokuza."

"Herm? Why not?"

I pointed to a corner of the screen at the caption *Exam for entrance.* It said, *Written exam with general common knowledge questions, plus interview by the club captain and some members.*

"Apparently, in order to get into this club, there's a written exam and an interview."

When I tapped my finger to indicate the relevant spots, Isshiki popped in from behind to peer at it with a disinterested *hmm*. "Ahhh, then he's got no chance, huhhh?"

"Ngh… Hachiman. I am mildly unskilled in interviews…"

"I know."

I knew it well… Well, it's not like I'm any good at interviews, either. I'd failed interviews for trivial part-time jobs without batting an eye, so never mind flaking out of a job—I've even ditched the interview before.

As my heart was dwelling on such personal failures to make the Hachiman of bygone days rapt with adoration, Isshiki reached all the way forward to do something on the laptop and made an *ahhh* sort of sound of understanding.

When I gave her a look that asked, *Was there something?* she gave me a little nod. "So then wouldn't that mean Yui would get in easy?"

"Huh? Why? I'm really bad at tests and stuff…" Yuigahama seemed surprised to hear her own name come up so suddenly. Blinking her big eyes, she looked at Isshiki.

Isshiki scrolled on down the screen. "Ah, no. The impression I get from the pictures on the site is that they let in folks looking to have a good time and meet hot girls, so I figure you'd get in easy."

"Oh, that does make sense," I said, nodding in response to Isshiki's remark. Written test aside, the interview seemed like something Yuigahama would be good at. She'd be able to establish rapport with that kind of party crowd, too.

Yuigahama appeared surprised to get a positive evaluation, as she blushed a little, smooshing her bun as she flicked glances over at me. "Y-you think?"

"Yeah, I bet you'd pick up on their annoying vibe real quick."

"That's your reason?! I take it back…" Yuigahama's shoulders dropped, and she jerked her face away.

Ah, not saying you're not cute! Please don't get it wrong. I just thought you would be able to keep up with these hype college students. It's just, I dunno. I think it may not be the best idea to blend into this particular crowd!

"Well, look. I mean, I'm sure they'd appreciate your looks, but it's what's on the inside that counts, you know… In fact, it's best not to join a club that decides its members based on looks and energy, probably. Not like I know."

"Huh? Hmm, well. That's. Yeah…" Yuigahama didn't seem quite convinced, but she reluctantly nodded, turning back to me.

Isshiki had been listening to the whole exchange. "You're really bad at backpedaling…," she said in exasperation.

Leave me alone. At least I can backpedal my way out of interviews for part-time jobs.

"What's on the inside, hmm…? If that's what we're talking about, what good would come from a gathering of people who all share the same opinion? You can't expect to grow in such a uniform, exclusive, and closed social situation…" Yukinoshita had been listening from the side, sounding skeptical as she gave the site a look.

Zaimokuza clapped his hands. "…Hpumf. So in other words, to make a comparison, it's like how a certain publishing giant monopolizes game magazines, making it hard for games created by other companies to get promoted, so the producer of a certain company refused to make a series into a game, citing this reason while simultaneously making a deal to make a game out of a different series from another publisher, which was a total flop…right?"

"That's too hard for me to understand, and I think you're talking about something completely different, but that's probably right." I went along with what he was saying, like, *Gotcha—which is short for I've got no idea what you're chattering on about,* and Zaimokuza gave me a solemn nod.

"I knew it! The Internet is where truth is found!"

Really? The Internet is so amazing. What kind of search do you have to do to reach that conclusion? What a search master. But I do feel that in the coming age, search experts will be needed. That's a modern sort of talent. I was actually impressed, in a way.

For some reason, a fiery fighting spirit was blazing up within Zaimokuza. "...Those fiends! So the fact that my talent lies undiscovered, that my debut was thwarted, was indeed the fault of that Empire of Evil, that certain publishing giant monopolizing the market!"

"Yeah, no."

Listen, just write it first, okay?

✕ ✕ ✕

After breaking for a debriefing, we once again gathered in front of the laptop.

Since *The Best or Bust! Kenken's Journal to Get That Top-Class Publishing Job Offer!* had not been very useful, we decided to try searching for something else that seemed good.

Of the various options, the job search websites had some pretty helpful information, like comments from people who were actually employed, plus selection criteria for companies and stuff.

And there, we found some shocking numbers.

"The acceptance rate at major publishers is insane...," I said. "Thousands of people apply and something like fifteen get in...?"

"The number of examinees isn't official, so we can't know hard numbers, but I would suppose the odds are roughly one in two to three hundred," Yukinoshita said, giving a general estimate.

Hearing her calculations, Yuigahama let out an impressed sigh. "Ohhh, it's tough to become an editor, huh?"

"And that's total number of hires, so if you also take into account the other departments, the number of people who can become editors gets even smaller."

Yukinoshita was right. Some people would be assigned to Operations or Sales, and there were different jobs within Editorial, too. There would only be one or two people assigned to the coveted light-novel editorial department in Zaimokuza's dreams. Worst case, new employees might not even be assigned there at all.

"M-mngh...," he moaned. "G-gnngh... So it would be easier to become a light-novel author..."

"Yeah, maybe." If you're talking purely about the acceptance rate, it seemed easier to debut on the writing side at Gagaga Bunko. It's not like there's an interview to become one.

I wanted the scoop on the acceptance rate of people debuting as light-novel authors from Gagaga Bunko, and I was reaching out to the computer to look it up when someone grabbed my hand from behind.

"H-hold on a sec there, please," Isshiki said with a shaking voice.

"Wh-what? What's wrong?" I asked.

With a trembling finger, looking quite desperate, she urged, "Mm! Mm!" pointing at the computer screen. "Look at this! Look!"

What...? I thought, and looking at the spot she indicated, I saw comments from employees of a certain publishing house, plus their job descriptions. It contained their universities, their daily responsibilities, an estimate of their weekly work hours and daily schedule, etc. Scanning down the list, my gaze stopped abruptly on one point.

"At age twenty-five, an annual income of a ten million yen..."

No way in hell. You've gotta be kidding. Wow. Publishing giants are something else... You can make that within three years of graduating? And then your income climbs, and you get it every year, right? Talk about a winner...

As I was trembling in shock, behind me, I heard a deep inhale and exhale. Glancing back, I saw Isshiki with her left hand on her cheek, a charming and cutesy smile on. "I'm going to marry an editor."

"Wait, wait, wait. Calm down. Hold on. *I'm* going to marry an editor."

"You're the one who needs to calm down...," Yukinoshita said, exasperated, and I gasped, snapping out of my trance.

So maybe I lost control a little. When you think about it, ten million yen isn't that big a deal. I'm *hachiman* myself, a value of eighty thousand yen, so that's roughly nothing more than 125 me's worth. Imagine how annoying it would be to have that many of me running around. Ten million is no big deal at all! Just one me is enough, and it's precisely because there's one of me that I have value!

As I was nodding to myself, winning myself over with mystery logic, Yuigahama was groaning. "Editor... An editor, huh...? Hmm..."

"Wellll, it's good to have a goal, *iiisn't* it?" said Isshiki. "I mean, until just now, I'd been working hard every day toward my goal."

"Your goal, huh...?" That wasn't very like Isshiki, and it bothered me. Wondering what her real motive was here, I looked over at her quizzically.

She touched her index finger to her jaw and gracefully tilted her head. "Of *cooourse*, it's to work for a few years before, like, quitting for marriage?"

"Just what part of that involves effort...?" Yukinoshita sighed.

Isshiki pouted huffily. "I mean, I'm not very good at school, and there isn't particularly anything I want to do..."

"I get that. I'm that type, too..." Yuigahama's shoulders slumped.

"Riiight?" Isshiki said. Something must have dawned on her, as her face jerked up, looking over at Yukinoshita. "Oh, but you seem like you'd work really hard."

Yukinoshita blinked in surprise. "I..." She trailed off, apparently having failed to anticipate that the conversation would be turned to her. Mouth open, she started to say something, but then her lips immediately drew tight.

Her long eyelashes pointed downward, and her hair spilled forward, revealing just a peek of her neck. Her white skin was so startling, I found myself gulping.

Her hands, laid politely over her skirt, moved just slightly, her fingers slowly closing into loose fists. "I don't know. I thought so before. But now...I don't know," she said, looking up, and then she smiled as if embarrassed.

"Well, that's fair enough. It's still down the road," Isshiki said lightly, and nobody spoke after that.

I think it was probably because neither I nor Yuigahama was listening to her.

Because Yukinoshita's answer was a little surprising.

There really aren't many high school students who can give a clear answer about their futures. But I'd had the vague idea that Yukinoshita had a solid idea about where she was headed. Or maybe that was just a selfish opinion I'd been projecting on her, but still, a strange sense of dissonance lay heavy in my heart.

With my elbow on the desk supporting my head, I was zoning out, watching Yukinoshita out of the corner of my eye when she noticed my gaze, cocking her head slightly with curiosity.

I gave a little shake of my head to imply it was nothing. She drew her chin back slightly and nodded.

...Well, she was still in her second year of high school, too. It wasn't strange for her to struggle to make decisions about her future. In fact, if she was avoiding making a statement precisely because of her lack of certainty, that reason made sense to me.

With that conclusion, I quelled my unease and turned my gaze forward again.

There my eyes met with Zaimokuza's, right in front of me, his arms crossed as he groaned, "What about you, Hachiman?"

"Hmm, me?"

"I think you're wasting your time asking Hikki..." Yuigahama gave me a chilly look.

I nodded back at her. "Yeah, you're right. My baseline is househusband."

"I knew it was pointless..." Yuigahama sighed, letting her head droop.

Yukinoshita closed her eyes, pressing her temple. "You should actually look up the meaning of *baseline*..."

Isshiki tapped my shoulder. I turned around to see her eyes sparkling, and then she cupped her hands around her mouth as if she were going to share a secret with me and whispered softly in my ear, "Becoming an editor is my recommendation for you. An editor."

"Nooope. Not working. Not getting a job," I answered, twisting around to escape the faint scent of Anna Sui and the tickle of her breath. "And it's not that easy to be an editor. Well, maybe if I started making a proper effort now, things could change."

"Hmm, must I begin now and put in years of effort...? What an arduous trial..." Zaimokuza gave a low honking moan as he held his head in his hands. But then his eyes flared wide, and he straightened his back. "...Then 'tis easiest to become a light-novel author after all! It's always been number one! Come, Hachiman! We have no time to waste! Let us set about my new book right away!"

Before he was even done with his outburst, Zaimokuza was sprinting toward the door. He came to a sliding stop there, then whirled around back to me. "Hachimaaaan! Pick up the pace!"

As he hopped on the spot, beckoning me, Zaimokuza looked like a repulsive creep, but when there was so much glee in his eyes, I almost broke out into a grin myself.

"Why don't you go?" Yukinoshita prompted me.

"Yeah," Yuigahama agreed. The smiles of both girls were distinctly forced.

"...Well, he is my case, after all," I said out loud to resign myself to the decision and stood.

Meanwhile, Irohasu was clacking away on the computer, looking up something. "You can make a free magazine pretty easy, riiight?"

You really have no interest in Zaimokuza...

×　　×　　×

The sky outside my window seat was blue and cloudless. Despite that, it was strangely lacking in warmth, and though the sky was clear, something about it was chilly. Or maybe this was due to the library atmosphere and the lack of background noise.

There was nobody but us in the hushed library after school. I'm sure there was someone somewhere behind the checkout desk supervising the place, but there was no sign of them.

Sitting diagonally opposite me, Zaimokuza had been scribbling away in his notebook with a mechanical pencil, but at some point, he'd stopped, too.

I wasn't sure if he'd lost steam or run out of ideas or what, but after sitting there staring into space for a while, he suddenly spoke up. "Herm, is there no use in becoming a light-novel author after all? ...I mean, I can't even marry a voice actress."

"Uhhh, if marrying a voice actress is a required part of the job, then most careers are out...," I said. "Same goes for editor, too."

"I see. So light-novel author shall not work, and 'tis impossible for an editor, too..." Zaimokuza moaned for a while, but then his eyes sparkled, and he shot to his feet in a *eureka!* moment.

"Bingo! So then in these times: director! I shall make an anime! Don-Don-Donuts, let's go nuts!" Zaimokuza's voice echoed through the quiet library.

When the reverberations faded, I couldn't stop a wry chuckle from escaping my lips. "...Well, as long as you're happy."

Zaimokuza blinked. "Hmm? Why are you talking to me like an ex-boyfriend…? H-hey, don't. We-we're not like that anymore…"

"Don't blush and get all flustered, creep. This is me throwing my hands up, you idiot. Just write. Or I can't go home."

"Hmm. That is so… I have no choice. I shall write." The excitement of his earlier cries was nowhere to be seen, and he was utterly awash in misery, his shoulders dejectedly hunching inward as he began writing in little dribs and drabs in his notebook.

Oh-ho, so he does intend to write a light novel. Surprising.

Though he didn't seem to exhibit any maturity, Zaimokuza was changing bit by bit. Even as he wandered down escape routes and side-tracks and detours and all sorts of paths, he was heading for his destination. It was too bad that the destination was just marrying a voice actress. Nevertheless, just as writing one character after another, one line after another, will eventually lead to finishing a book, each day passes until the time comes when you go out into the world.

There was one more year until I would graduate high school. If I'm to assume that after that, I would make it into university just fine, then graduate without a hitch, there were only five more years until I went out into society as an adult.

Five years.

It felt like both an extraordinarily long time and the blink of an eye. I think as I grow older, the period of one year will become shorter and shorter. A year's time right now wasn't going to be the same as next year or the year after.

And I'm sure its value will be different, too.

Maybe even this hopeless time spent just looking up at the chilly sky has value.

I think right now, I'll keep gazing at this beautiful dry sky for a while.

Surely, **Iroha Isshiki** is made of sugar and spice and everything nice.

The heater was rattling.

The one installed in the clubroom was pretty old, and something always went wrong with it if you left it running too long. Was the fan stuck? Or was there some problem with the motor? Or maybe the frame was twisted?

After school, around sunset, our club's heater-chan had started to make these very quiet little noises, as if letting us know she was reaching her limit.

When I was focused on reading or when the girls were talking, it didn't bother me much. But the moment things went quiet, I could make it out.

Her eyes down on her paperback, Yukinoshita paused her hand in turning a page, then looked over to the heater by the window. It seemed to have caught her attention, too. "...Seems more quiet than usual, hmm."

"Yeah. It's kinda calming." Yuigahama looked up from her phone and reached out to her mug.

I followed suit, picking up my traditional-style cup as well, chugging the black tea that was no longer steaming.

Yuigahama and I both expelled sighs of satisfaction, and then once again, in the silence, there came the little rattle. Even Yuigahama must have noticed it, as she glanced over to the heater.

Isshiki had been showing up to the clubroom with increasing frequency, so maybe that was why we hadn't much noticed the noises coming from the heater.

It was not that Isshiki was always loud or talkative or made a racket, but simply that when she was gone, her absence turned our attention to other things. I mean, when Isshiki came around, she was generally bringing some dumb issue with her, so naturally, it made things in here more hectic.

Thanks to her, it had been some time since it was so quiet in here.

While enjoying the warm tea and snacks, I distractedly read my book, listening to the sound of one calm voice and one cheerful one chatting in the background, and occasionally joining the conversation.

We had no guests and no work to do—even time was slow. Once you got used to it, it was just an inconsequential, mundane routine, but it had been a while since we'd fallen back on it. It was rather nice. The noises from the heater were almost charming somehow, like the rhythmic patter of rain.

I closed my book, listening to the heater doing its best, and looked over to the window.

As I was gazing at the sunset and zoning out, Yukinoshita started to talk again. "Then how about we call it a day?"

"Yeah, it doesn't look like anyone's coming," Yuigahama replied. "Last cookie's mine!" she chirped and started cleaning up the snacks.

Yukinoshita and I got ready to go, then took care of the last sweep to make sure the room was ready to be locked. While checking to make sure the windows were closed, I reached out to the heater switch. "You did good today," I said, then flicked off the power, and the rattling stopped. It was going to be cold for a while, so it'd be a good idea to tell Miss Hiratsuka about this to get the heater inspected or fixed.

Wrapping ourselves in our coats and scarves, the three of us went out into the hallway. Yukinoshita locked the door of the clubroom.

Now business was closed for the day.

With work over, all that was left was to return home. When we stepped out from the clubroom into the hallway of the special-use building, Yuigahama shivered, pulling together the front of her coat. "…It's freezing out here! It's so cold in the hallway!"

The emptiness of the passageway alone was enough to create a chill. It was as if the cold air was rising up from the floor. I wrapped my scarf tighter. "It's 'cause the clubroom was warm. It makes you feel colder."

"There's no heating out here." Yukinoshita strode off, implying that we just needed to shake it off.

Lining up beside her, Yuigahama stroked her scarf, a rather pensive look on her face. "Hmm… Oh, I know!" she piped up, leaping on Yukinoshita and clinging to her arm. "Maybe this'll warm us up!"

"H-hey, Yuigahama." Yukinoshita swayed, and her tone was a little sharp, with a protest in her gaze. But seeing Yuigahama's warm and fuzzy expression, she sighed in resignation.

"…Ohhh, you're so warm!"

"It's hard to walk…"

I don't think the temperature had changed much, but the apparent temperature seemed to be higher. Just seeing their exchange did make me warmer, actually!

Even after Yukinoshita was done returning the key to the teachers' room, Yuigahama was glued to her hip. Following the two girls wrapped around each other, I went on down the hallway to the front entrance, where a familiar face emerged from the student council room.

"Huh? It's Iroha-chan. Yahallo!" Her right hand still coiled around Yukinoshita's arm, Yuigahama gave a little wave with her left hand.

Isshiki trotted over. "Ohhh, hellooo! Good thing you're still here!"

"We were just about to leave," Yukinoshita said, with Yuigahama still attached to her. I feel like an outsider would be really weirded out and think, *What's with all the flirting...?*

But of course, this was Isshiki. Maybe she was just used to it, as she didn't seem bothered at all, replying calmly as usual. "I was just finishing up now, so I was thinking I'd stop by for a bit."

"Did you have some kind of business?" I asked her.

"Yes, as a matter of fact!" Isshiki nodded. She glanced at the girls like she was concerned about something, then beckoned me with a tiny gesture. "Heeey, do you have a minute?"

"Huh? Uhhh...sure..." I looked over to Yukinoshita and Yuigahama, signaling to go on without me, and both of them nodded. Isshiki tugged me along by the sleeve to the edge of the hallway, by the window.

The sky had dimmed to a darker shade, and the wind hitting the glass seemed icy. With her back to the glass, Isshiki seemed a little hesitant. "Um, what about that job I asked you about before? I'd like an answer soon..."

"Mm, yeah. I'll do it. I'll figure it out."

Upon hearing *job*, I reflexively gave her the standard answer of a corporate cog: apparent eagerness, if nothing else. I didn't want her talking to me about work as I was leaving. The Service Club was done with business for the day. I wanted her to leave that sort of thing for another time. It was cold, and I wanted to go home now.

After giving her that slimy reply, I turned around—but then Isshiki called to me from behind. "Oh, really? So then is ten tomorrow at Chiba Station good?"

"Huh? Tomorrow?" I turned back to her on instinct.

That was the weekend. The Hikigaya household has a biweekly break—meaning two days off a week. A day off is a day off. The issue is the Service Club also had a biweekly break—but biweekly in the "once every two weeks" definition. *Biweekly* can mean different things, you know. There's a nugget of knowledge for you. In other words, if she was saying *work* in the Service Club sense, then even if it was the weekend, I could be forced into business. If you really think about it, that's not even a biweekly break. What's with this exploitative club…?

"Uh, I can't really tomorrow…" I would give a random excuse in order to secure my weekend.

Isshiki stuck her finger on her chin and cocked her head cutely. "But you know tomorrow's free, right?"

"How should I know…?"

I always wondered why Isshiki kept talking under the assumption that I would be aware of things she'd never told me. *I'm not aware of your plans or whatever. I don't know everything. I just know what I know.*

Isshiki puffed up her cheeks in that calculating way of hers. "But we're talking about you here."

"Me…? Uh, that makes less sense. Well, it's true I'm free…"

"I kneeew it. See ya tomorrow! I'm looking forward to your being hard at work! Buh-bye!"

"O-okay…"

Isshiki beamed at me, ending the discussion, then waved bye-bye.

Nooo! Irohasu has such a nice smile! Not only can I not refuse her, I feel like I'm not even allowed to ask questions or inquire about details!

Ah, crap! Did I promise something…? She said it was for a job… I bet she asked me to do something…but it doesn't ring any bells…

Somehow that smile felt like a physical shove in the direction of the front entrance.

After a few steps forward, I turned to look back at Isshiki, but she still had that same grin plastered on her face and continued to wave at me.

Well, this was me we were talking about. There was the possibility I'd said whatever it took to get away from her. In fact, that's the only possibility. The issue was the promise itself…

I just couldn't remember. Burying my face in my scarf as I mumbled to myself in muffled grunts, I considered various potential options, but I just couldn't think of it.

As I racked my brain, I arrived at the entrance, where I saw Yukinoshita and Yuigahama standing there talking. I'd made them wait, hadn't I?

"Ack, sorry. You could've just gone without me…," I said, and Yuigahama spun around to face me. The momentum yanked on Yukinoshita's hand, which was still in her grasp. *This is just like when you take a pampered dog that drags you around on a walk.*

"Oh, we weren't really waiting for you. Yukinon and I were talking, and we just kinda wound up staying behind…right?" Yuigahama turned to ask Yukinoshita, who stuck her nose in the air.

"…That's right." Yukinoshita somehow looked like a cat that didn't appreciate being held.

"All right. Well, uh…thanks anyway." When I expressed my gratitude, they gave little shakes of their heads. That very trivial gesture was weirdly embarrassing to me, so I slipped my feet into my loafers and walked on out.

When we emerged outside, it was already dark. Though it was almost spring by the lunar calendar, it would be some time until the days got longer.

As I headed from the entrance to the front gate, Yuigahama trotted up beside me. "What did Iroha-chan say?"

"Uh, I don't really know… She has some job, but the details are lost on me…"

"That explanation tells us nothing…," Yukinoshita commented with exasperation and a smile as she came up one step behind me.

But with work, you don't often get much of an explanation. The fact was that our activities as the Service Club thus far had been largely without any details… We had experienced one too many situations where things would have gone smoother if we'd just gotten an explanation to begin with, and now I felt like, you know, reports, communication, and discussion were important.

Taken from another angle: If you just do your reporting and communicating and discussing, you can even flake out on doing the work itself. And if the higher-ups complain, you can worm your way out of responsibilities by snapping back at them like, *But I already filed reports and communicated and discussed this with you!*

I was ready to wiggle out of the job tomorrow using these tactics!

✕   ✕   ✕

It was the weekend on a clear winter day. Chiba Station was buzzing with people. It probably wasn't nearly as bad as Tokyo, but I wasn't used to going out on weekends, so it seemed plenty crowded to me.

Watching the people rushing in front of the station in my peripheral vision, I checked the time: 10:05. It was past the appointed time, yet there was still no sign of Isshiki. Unfortunately, I didn't know her number to check with her, either.

If we're meeting in front of the station, you'd assume it's at the east entrance, but maybe she's gone to the other one...? Or maybe she's at Keisei Chiba Station. I mean, it used to be called National Railway Chiba Eki-mae Station Your Guess Is as Good as Mine... That was the name... And even aside from one of the original Chiba stations, there's also Nishi Chiba, Higashi Chiba, and Hon Chiba, and Chiba Minato, Chiba Kouen, Chiba Chuo, and even Chiba New Town... There's so many station names and train lines with Chiba in them. The bar was too high for a Chiba beginner.

Whether you're a resident of Chiba prefecture or Chiba city, "going to Chiba" almost certainly indicates going to Chiba Station, but maybe it's hard for people of other regions to get the hint. If someone from Hokkaido says *I'm going to Hokkaido*, I'm sure everyone else would wonder what they're on, and if a Tokyoite says *I'm going to Tokyo*, you kinda get the feeling they're heading out to follow their dreams and make it big.

I was right to wait for her here, since she'd told me to meet at the station. I was stepping in place to ward off the cold as I waited, when I discovered Isshiki among the crowds.

Her beige coat was tightly closed in front, and she wore a fur scarf. Her pleated skirt was short, but she was wearing boots, so she didn't look cold. Her heels were a little on the tall side and clicked as she walked.

When she noticed me, she trotted my way, tightening her scarf and fiddling with her bangs, then took a breath and flashed her face up toward me. "Sorry for making you wait. I had to get ready…"

"Took you long enough." *Irohasu, you're so laaaate.*

Isshiki's response to my complaint was huffy sulking. "I think this is the part where you say, 'I just got here'… I mean, since we're about to go on a date."

"…A date?"

There's a word I'm not used to hearing…

I think a date is a ceremony where you make a raging spirit all lovey-dovey ushy-gushy and stuff to pacify its wrath… And then at the end, there's a battle! I think. No, wait, scratch that last one. If you just think about it like a normal person, a date is that thing where a guy and girl go hang out together.

But then why would I suddenly be hanging out with Isshiki…?

I must have been an open book, as Isshiki put a hand to her waist as if to say, *Good grief.* She let out a little sigh. "I *tooold* you to come up with a plan for this date, didn't I?"

"…Ohhh." *Now that she mentions it, she did say something about that last month. I guess she was actually serious?*

I seemed to recall giving her some noncommittal response like *I'll think about it.* How careless! I can't believe she got that pledge out of me!

"If that's the case, I wish you'd just tell me from the start. I need to do stuff to get ready for these things…you know?"

For example, I could have squeezed in some other plans so I could refuse, or never decided on a day and put it off for the rest of my life, or gotten a stomachache on the day of. There were a number of things I could have done. Well, I got the feeling that the end result would be the same even if she had told me ahead of time. And do you always feel like canceling on the day of an event, even when you've been looking forward to it?

Isshiki was unfazed by my vehement arguments and attempts to resist, and her attitude remained the same. "I mean, if I had invited you out normally, you wouldn't come."

"…Well, that's true." She's good. If she understood me to that degree, she could pass about level 3 of the Hikigaya Certification Exam.

Regardless, it was due to my own shortcoming that she'd managed to get a commitment out of me. Even if I made excuses for myself now, nothing would let us part ways on the spot. I had brought about this situation by not thinking critically and replying recklessly. It was fair to say it would be irresponsible to abandon this now.

The optimal plan would be to get this over with as quickly as possible and go home.

"Let's go," I said.

"Yep, let's." Isshiki nodded, then finally smiled at me.

"So where are we going?"

As soon as I said that, Isshiki frowned. Letting out a deep, deep sigh, she pouted grumpily. "*Aghh…* Is that my responsibility now…? I thought you'd think that stuff up for me …"

"When I'm out on my own, I get excited to map out my day, but when I'm with someone else, my MO is to follow their lead."

"Whatever… Let's think about it as we walk! It's cold here." Isshiki's shoulders drooped in resignation, but then she immediately fixed up her scarf as if energizing herself again and set off, heels clicking.

Mm-hmm, looks like Irohasu has gotten used to the way I do things.

By the way, which of us was just made to wait out here in the cold, huh…?

X   X   X

We headed down the long street that led from the station to the central downtown area.

This was the part of Chiba you could call the main street, lined with restaurants, entertainment businesses, and commercial buildings, and on the weekends, there were a lot of people strolling along the sidewalk. Students often stopped by here on weekday evenings, too, so I was familiar with the area.

If we continued ahead, we'd reach an area I often frequented with a movie theater, a bookstore, and an arcade. Turn left ahead, and there was a PARCO department store. If you're going to hang around the Chiba area, this was the street to visit. It seemed a lot of people were on the same wavelength, because it had heavy foot traffic, as usual.

Though I was used to wandering this street, having a girl next to me made it an unfamiliar and confusing experience. I suppose walking side by side would be the natural thing to do, but my feet couldn't help but rush, and if I didn't make a conscious effort, I'd find myself leaving her behind. Blowing out a shallow breath to calm my nerves, and keeping in mind to go slower than my usual pace, I walked about half a step ahead of Isshiki.

As we made our way along, avoiding the passersby, her footsteps sped up to pull alongside me. She leaned forward slightly to look up at me. "Hey, what sort of places do you go to normally?"

"Home."

"Try again."

"O-okay…"

Isshiki's tone was quite a bit sharper than usual as she shot me a withering look.

Iroha-chan, you're freaking me out…! Intimidated by how quiet she was, I cleared my throat and offered a new answer. "The library or a bookstore, I guess. They let me kill time, and they're just fun."

"A library date…," she muttered with a tilt of her head, looking up at the sky. She seemed to be considering for a while, but her head quickly lowered again in apology. "Sorry, but I associate that more intellectual stuff with Hayama. I wanted something crappier from you."

Harumph, this brat… Look at my grades. I can be the intellectual type, you know? Well, I don't want to go to the library with Isshiki, either, so whatever.

I was already a little nervous, so if I went someplace quiet with her, I seriously didn't think I could keep it together. I thought I'd wind up feeling like a dad who wants to take it easy over the weekend but ends up having to watch his whining kids. And on the topic of the library, if I went to one with Hayama, I felt like I would be able to calmly read a book. Uh-oh! Here I am, imagining going on a library date with Hayama! Yeeeek! If Ebina could read my thoughts, it'd be a disaster! No, but actually.

I didn't really care too much about Hayama, so for the time being, let's chase him out from that corner of my mind forever.

Racking my brain, I wondered what other places would be socially acceptable for hanging out.

"Karaoke, darts, billiards, bowling, Ping-Pong… You could go to a batting cage, but there isn't one around the Chiba Station area…" *Anything pique your interest?* I asked her with a look.

Isshiki looked very serious. "I know this doesn't matter, but billiards doesn't suit you."

"Leave me alone."

"Oh, but Ping-Pong would!"

"That doesn't make me feel better…"

Like, there was something malicious in the way she said that… Ping-Pong is super-cool. Haven't you heard of Matsumoto's *Ping Pong*? The manga and the anime were real cool.

While we were talking, we arrived at the big five-way intersection and stopped at the light. Turn left from here, and that goes toward the PARCO. If you go straight ahead, you'll hit the movie theater. There's nothing of note if you turn right, so it would be one of the first two.

"…Anyway, is a movie okay? We can kill two hours," I suggested.

"Why are you assuming we're killing time…? Well, I'll leave it to you…"

"Then a movie it is."

Despite Isshiki's grumbling, she'd given me the okay, so I stepped toward the movie theater.

Being that it was a weekend, it was doing good business.

As I browsed the screenings and checked the available seats, Isshiki pointed to a poster for a Hollywood blockbuster. The huge tagline said it was an Academy Award–nominated movie. "I want to see this one."

"Okay. And I'll go see this one." My movie of choice had no relation to any Academy Awards. The screening time for both films was about the same. It didn't seem like one of us would have to wait too long for the other movie to finish.

"All we have to do is decide on a meeting spot," I said. "Is the Starbucks on the floor below okay?"

By nature, I'm not in the habit of watching movies with others, so I thought I was making the obvious choice. In fact, I thought I was being considerate by taking the running times into account, so then *whyever* would Iroha-chan be staring at me with her mouth hanging open?

"…Huh? What?" I asked.

Isshiki nodded to herself as if it all made sense to her now. "I *seeee*. This behavior is the cause of everything, huhhh?"

Not sure what conclusions she's drawing, but I'm just honored she understands me!

Isshiki let out a short sigh of exasperation and looked away from the screen with the previews. And then, she fixed her eyes on one point.

Following her gaze, I saw the sign of a bowling alley. Below it was something mentioning Ping-Pong tables.

After considering that sign, Isshiki spun back around to face me. "Actually, why don't we drop the movie and play Ping-Pong?"

"Works for me, but won't you have trouble in those shoes?" I asked, looking at Isshiki's boots, and she stopped on the spot, examined her own feet, then glanced up at my face.

When she stared at me with her slack jaw and dumb expression, her innocence reminded me that she was younger than me.

She seemed like she wanted to say something.

"Wh-what?" I asked.

"Nothing… I'm just surprised you noticed…"

"Your eye level was higher than usual. I could tell that much."

Isshiki took one step toward me as if to expressly check that, facing me. When I took a step back, her eyebrows knitted, and she came another step closer. That seemed to imply that I shouldn't move. I leaned back slightly, and she peered up at me. Then her full lips split into a grin. "Oh, you're right. You're closer than usual," she observed eloquently.

Our faces were far closer than normal, and it made me realize just how glossy her lips were as she smiled, and I couldn't stop myself from gulping.

When I failed to speak, even she must have felt flustered by the closeness, as her cheeks went pink, and she averted her eyes. She timidly peeked back at me, putting on a bashful act.

"…Well, you can rent shoes, I guess." I looked away from her, striding toward the bowling alley.

"Right." Isshiki scampered after me.

This girl can be so manipulative…

Even so, the worst part was that she was still cute.

Her face was, in fact, cute. Though her gestures were calculated, they were still adorable. And when it came to her personality, even though I feel like there were some defects, you could call it cute how she tried to weaponize her cuteness.

Man. The hell. She *is* cute. It wouldn't even be weird if she introduced herself as *the school idol!! Iroha-chaaan!* …No, I take that back. That would be weird.

However, neither her cunning nor her cuteness was directed at me—they were aimed past me, at Hayato Hayama, and that was what enabled me to maintain a certain level of cool. If I'd had to deal with this back in my pure and innocent phase, I'd have been knocked out in one shot, y'all…

Deliberately putting on a pseudo-Kansai accent brought me face-to-face with my identity as a Chibanese. Reaffirming my love for my hometown, as well as my own standpoint, calmed me down. *That was close—if not for my love for Chiba, I'd have been utterly defeated by Irohasu's wiles. Thanks, Chiba. I heart Chiba.*

As I collected myself, I recalled my goal for the day. I'd been assigned the task of coming up with a date plan for her and Hayama.

I turned back to check with Isshiki as we left the station mall hallway and the bowling alley came into view.

"But, like, does Hayama even play Ping-Pong? Wouldn't some fancy-schmancy sort of place be better?"

"That's what makes this gooood! If we just go to his usual haunts, that wouldn't set me apart from other girls, riiight?"

"I see…" Now that she pointed it out, yeah. Miura, who Isshiki would see as her current rival, probably wouldn't invite Hayama to Ping-Pong. In that sense, Isshiki would be setting herself apart…though who knows if that was negative or positive. And Hayama doesn't seem like the type to see any difference in the first place…

Well, this is to help my cute junior. Guess I'll give it my best shot.

X   X   X

The bowling alley wasn't far from the movie theater. We paid at the front, then headed to the Ping-Pong table in the corner. At the leather sofa off to the side, I changed my shoes. Sitting beside me, Isshiki removed her coat as well and began changing her shoes.

The pink knit sweater under her coat emphasized the girlish lines of her body, which was slender and modest, and her high skirt showed off the nip of her waist. When she violently yanked off her boots, I could tell how shapely her calves were even through her tights.

There was a sort of lingering childishness to her gestures, and I couldn't help but watch—and then our eyes met, and Isshiki tilted her head as if to ask if something was up. Of course I couldn't say that I'd been captivated by the mismatch between her charm and innocent body language, so with a little shake of my head, I wordlessly offered her a paddle.

Isshiki bobbed her head and accepted it, then fanned herself with it as she stood in front of the Ping-Pong table. "I haven't played this game since middle school gym class."

"When you're in your second year, you can opt into it."

I stood in front of Isshiki with the table between us. She rolled up the sleeves of her sweater and pointed her paddle at me. And then she gave me the kind of bold grin that made me feel uncomfortable… Guess there's two sweaters in here now!

"All right," she said, "how about we say that if I win, you treat me to lunch?"

"We're betting lunch? Sure, I guess…," I answered, tossing the Ping-Pong ball over to Isshiki. If we were going to be having a match anyway, then a wager would add a bit of excitement to it.

The Ping-Pong ball bounced on the table with its characteristic hollow *pok*, and then she snatched it up and raised her paddle. "Then it's settled! …My serve fiiirst! Hyah," she called out lazily. There was a *badonk* as the ball hopped weakly toward me.

"Hup." I tapped the ball back, not hitting it any harder than necessary. It fell perfectly in front of Isshiki, bouncing just to the right height.

"Tah." She returned the ball.

The Ping-Pong ball went back and forth awhile. *Badunk, badonk.*

The sound really took me back. When my family had gone to hot springs in the past, I'd often played with Komachi. That had gotten me good at cooperating with your opponent to keep a rally going. I'd mastered it with *Mario Kart* and *Puyo Puyo*, too. I mean, since Komachi can be a sore loser…

Just like when I played against Komachi, I continued to hit the ball back into spots that would be as easy for Isshiki to return.

"Tah."

"Hup."

We called out lethargically as the Ping-Pong ball bounced across the table. It seemed that one of my 108 Big Brother Skills, "Entertaining the Little Sister," had not gotten rusty.

Though Isshiki's returns started off timid, she gradually picked up speed. Right as I was starting to enjoy this, I saw a suspicious flash in her eye.

As the ball boinged upward, she locked in on it, then took a step forward, and with a big windup, she swung hard. "DIIIE!"

"Uh, that was weird…"

The ball Isshiki had struck flew in a big arc, disappearing with a twinkle into the distance. For some reason, Irohasu was triumphantly

saying "How about that?!" with a satisfied smile... Table tennis does not have home runs.

I went to go pick up the ball and restart from my serve, but then due to a stupid slipup of mine, it was Isshiki's turn to serve again.

"My serve then, huh?"

Ponk, ponk went the ball as she bounced it on the table, preparing to serve. That was when she seemed to realize something, looking all around and then popping up a hand to call for a time-out. "Ah, hold on for a sec— HYAH!" She abandoned her call to stop and then suddenly launched it at me with full power.

Don't think I can't see through your little act. I calmly circled around in front of the ball and fired back with an unreturnable strike in the opposite direction of her step inward. "...Nice try."

When I was younger, my dad had gotten me with the same techniques every time we played Ping-Pong. As revenge, I'd subjected Komachi to them a handful of times, and she'd really hated me for it! You can't underestimate the badness genes of the Hikigaya family line! Little Komachi had burst into tears and gone, *I'm never playing Ping-Pong with you ever again, Bro!* which was too cute...

Komachi had still been small then, so she had really cried her eyes out. But looking over at my current partner, wondering how it would be for grown-up Irohasu, I saw her clenching her teeth in frustration over the failure of her ploy.

"Ngh..."

"If you're gonna use moves like that, then I'll have to kick it into high gear...," I warned, flinging off my jacket. And with a squeak of rubber against the floor, I adopted a stance like a Ping-Pong pro.

With a swing of her paddle, Isshiki protested, "H-hey! You're being childish!"

"Says you... Whatever, let's go. My serve."

This was nothing like my earlier cooperative act. I'd been holding back. This time, I smashed the ball with full force, aiming for the corner of the Ping-Pong table. For someone who had been whining and griping about it, Isshiki sure seemed to be into this, as a short grunt slipped out of her as she scrambled for the ball.

"Hrya!" When her paddle whiffed through empty air, the added momentum made Isshiki's skirt flutter.

Oh, crap. Now that I think about it, she's in a skirt... I should avoid hitting back so fast...

After that, I decided to dial it back a bit, hitting on the light side, but now that I was aware of it, I couldn't stop thinking about it, and my gaze kept being drawn down like gravity. I couldn't stop glancing at the flapping of Isshiki's skirt.

Ngh! Unfair!

Just what was so unfair? The table was in the way, and I couldn't see anything! The hell, something was seriously wrong with this sport!! ... Oh, I know, if they invented a Ping-Pong table that was made of transparent *I-can-see-right-through-you* material, it'd even turn into a fad. Actually, I should invent it and get rich quick.

Maybe it was because I was entertaining stupid thoughts or I was hypnotized by her skirt, but my paddle kept slicing through air, and Isshiki kept racking up points.

She let out a breath and pulled a mini towel from her bag to daintily dab at her sweat before she started to count off on her fingers. "Ummm, you have eight points now, and my score is one, two, three, four... Oh, what time is it right now?"

I felt like I'd heard this one before, but I obliged, looking over at the clock on the wall. "Eleven."

"Eleven. Is that right? Oh, right. My score. Twelve, thirteen."

"Start at six. Six points."

That's some really blatant Toki Soba there. Just how much is this girl going to fudge the numbers? Well, she's a woman of culture, knowing classic rakugo.

When I pointed this out, Isshiki gave me a sulky pout, but it was ineffective.

"C'mon, let's go," I called out, firing off a serve that was on the more relaxed side. Though I was holding back on speed, I aimed for a difficult spot on the table. Isshiki pattered over, but the ball mercilessly bounced away, loudly projecting off the corner.

After watching it go, Isshiki turned back to me with a bright smile. "Ah, that was out, so that's my point, huh?"

"If it were out, then it wouldn't bounce or make a sound…"

How can she lie through her teeth…?

And haven't you been pulling some unfair moves? Like…I think your skirt puts me at a disadvantage!

After that, I scored most of the points, occasionally getting distracted by her skirt and making more mistakes, until finally, the game came to a close.

If we're just talking results, then it was a crushing win for me.

The game over, the two of us fwumped down on the nearby sofa. It had been such a long time since I'd played Ping-Pong, and I was almost panting.

Isshiki, on the other hand, was stricken by the shock of her loss and sat with slumped shoulders, crestfallen. …*You still have a long way to go!*

"…Can we agree I won?" I confirmed.

Isshiki reluctantly nodded. "Oh well… We can call it my loss, this time…" Despite having pulled so many dirty moves, she acknowledged her loss with unexpected honesty. If this had been a certain other sore loser, then she almost certainly would have played until she won.

I'm not the type to fixate on competitions, but it doesn't feel bad to win. A nasty smirk grew on my face despite myself, but when I looked at Isshiki, I couldn't bring myself to laugh in her face.

I cleared my throat to get the chuckle under control. "Thanks for lunch." I tried to keep it light.

Isshiki was still hanging her head, and her shoulders trembled slightly. *…H-huh? I didn't make Irohasu cry, did I? Ah, ah, wh-what do I do…?*

As I was getting panicked and flustered, I heard a low chuckle from beside me. "…Heh-heh-heh."

Looking over, I saw Isshiki raise her head, an intrepid smile on her face.

"Huh, what? What is it?"

She put a hand on her waist, and with a triumphant expression, she pointed at me. "I did say that if I win, then you would treat me, but I never said I'd treat you if *you* won."

What is she talking about…? I thought, giving her a dubious look. But then I remembered before our game. *…Huhhh?*

"……You're right."

Isshiki had only set out a condition for her own victory… She's good. This has been an educational experience… I'll use this on Komachi the next time we have a competition over something. Thinking about finally earning Komachi's disgust again, I couldn't restrain the pounding of my heart…

Anyway, this Irohasu—she really was terrible in both word and deed. "Well, I never really expected you to treat me to begin with, but isn't this kind of sneaky…?" I asked, a little sharply.

Isshiki was about as unconcerned as you could get. In fact, she only smiled gently back at me. She lightly laid a hand on her chest, leaning over just a tad to peer at my face. Her eyes seemed to be teasing me. "Aren't girls supposed to be a little sneaky?"

"Well, all right…" I was exasperated, but I couldn't really argue.

I think it was Mother Goose or something that had that rhyme about girls being made of sugar and spice and everything nice.

It was true. Though I get the feeling Isshiki got a bit too much spice.

"…Whatever. That argument won't work on all boys, okay? Especially when pulling stuff like today."

There were people out there who were serious about games, who would get legitimately angry when they lost at Millionaire, and who were the target of all the jokes.

Well, guys like Hayama and Tobe would lighten up the vibe, and with Isshiki's looks and communication skills, I think she'd be forgiven in most cases. I mean, even I'm forgiving her, after all!

It seemed Isshiki figured out what I was trying to say, and her expression suddenly turned meek. She waved her hands rapidly as if to say there was no way. "No, no, no, of course, there's no way I'd do that in front of Hayama! What if he hated me for it?!"

"…Well, I think he'd like you more if you did."

"For real? Where'd you get that info, huh?!"

"No particular source."

Isshiki suddenly leaned forward enthusiastically, so I shifted a proportionate distance to the side. When I did, Isshiki approached no further, folding her arms as she began to consider. "Hmm… An uncertain source won't count as evidence… It doesn't seem I can execute that plan yet."

"It's not like you have to rush things. Right now, he—," I began, when Isshiki, who had been gradually inching toward me, cut me off.

"So then for now…" She paused there before moving her lips close to my ear, softly and secretively, and then adding one more thing—

A pinch of spice all rolled up in sugar.

"…I only do this sort of thing to you."

"I'm just gonna take that to mean you don't care if I hate you…," I muttered, leaning away from her, and Isshiki giggled.

No matter how much sugar you sprinkled on it, a habanero is a habanero. And even if you drizzled syrup on it, Tabasco is Tabasco.

It doesn't come together without that "everything nice."

✕   ✕   ✕

A certain amount of exercise is guaranteed to make you hungry.

When we left the bowling alley, Isshiki, walking beside me, came to tap-tap on my shoulder. "*Heeey*, aren't you hungryyy?"

"Hmm, yeah. You wanna get something?" I turned around to answer.

"Yeah." She flashed me a smile, but she didn't offer anything more.

Wait, is this what I think it is? Do I have to ask? The question…

I steeled myself, then said with great trepidation, "…What do you wanna eat?"

"I don't care."

I—I knew it! She's one of those people who claims she doesn't care when you're trying to pick somewhere to eat!

I've heard rumors on the wind that girls of society measure the quality of a boy based on his suggestion. The boy is put on trial… But I will say this:

The secret to success may be the awareness that just as a boy is tested by a girl, we are also in the position of testing a girl.

And I will offer you these words:

"When you gaze long into the abyss, the abyss also gazes into you."

—Nietzsche

Whoops, seeing that The Best or Bust! Kenken's Journal to Get That Top-Class Publishing Job Offer! *the other day got me all pretentious for a second there… Gotta pull myself together and face reality.*

Not so long ago, Isshiki's question would have made me dissolve into anger and go Super Saiyan, but my recent experiences had turned me into an adult.

"How about pasta? Or *arrabbiata*? Or *tagliata*?"

"Why are all those pasta…?"

"*Tagliata* isn't pasta." It's a dish of sliced beef.

My manner of speaking must have irritated her, as her eyebrows twitched for a second. I could count on her to maintain that smile.

Even if she was smiling on the surface, it seemed in the depths of her heart, she was annoyed. In a soft but sharp voice, she muttered, "…I've always known you were a terrible person."

"Right back atcha."

Isshiki put her index finger to her jaw and did this cute tilt of her head as if to say she had no clue. "But everyone always says I'm so charming?"

Her ability to say that with such a nonchalant look spoke to a strong heart. Yeah, she's a real charmer all right. If we're just talking mental fortitude, she's stronger than the Japan National rugby team…

As we strolled along, I considered our options. "If you're fine with anything, then…Saize."

Isshiki shook her head no. *I thought you were fine with anything…* It seemed I'd have to come up with an answer that intuited her desires somewhat.

So began *Quiz! Guess Irohasu's Lunch!* Now I would have to bring up a string of contenders that seemed like they would satisfy Isshiki.

"Then we could go with Jolly-Pasta."

Isshiki turned her face away as if to say, *Non.*

Wrong answer, huh…? "Ngh, fine, I'll compromise and go with Kabe no Ana."

She tilted her head as if to say, *Pardon?*

Nghhh, is there any other pasta restaurant…? "W-would Capricciosa be okay?"

Finally, Isshiki sighed. It seemed my time was up. I got no answers correct in *Quiz! Guess Irohasu's Lunch!* and scored zero points. "Those were all totally pasta related... I'm fine with wherever you want to go."

"For real? You're okay if it's not pasta or avocado?"

"Seriously, what do you take me for...?" Isshiki glared at me.

I mean, girls liked pasta and avocado... Also shrimp. Or that's the impression I get. I bet they would love a Cobb pasta salad, which would have both avocado and pasta. Best thing since sliced bread, right?

Though she was saying she was fine with the restaurant of my choosing, she'd just rejected Saize. So just in case, I made sure to check one more time. "You're really okay with that? You're not trying to test me?" I asked.

She looked away, gazing contemplatively at nothing. "Well, normally, I would be doing that now, but..."

So she does normally do that... Irohasu can be scary.

"But today I'm fine with your choice."

...That's a relief. I mean, the only other pasta place I know would just be Tapas & Tapas, though there isn't one close to Chiba Station.

I guess I should take her to one of my usual spots.

But of course, a mere high schooler wouldn't have much in the way of regular spots, so that automatically narrowed down my contenders. You would expect family restaurants and cafés to be really crowded around this time on weekends. Then again, it wasn't like I knew anything about fancy-schmancy or high-class restaurants.

If I were to borrow what Isshiki had said that day: She was expecting something crappy from me.

That left one answer.

"Okay, then I guess we'll go there...," I said, walking one step ahead of Isshiki to show the way. I headed off for the center of Chiba.

At Chiba Station, there are food establishments clustered in the malls like Sogo, PARCO, and C-one and on the main streets, but there were more businesses on the road that's nicknamed Nanpa Street, as well as the narrow alley that runs parallel to it.

In fact, when you get to be a Chibanese of my level, you make the deliberate choice to go down that alley for holes-in-the-wall. Normally, I'd try to discover someplace new, but on that day, I had company. It was probably best to select a more popular location.

When we went out onto the street, the orange sign of the restaurant came into view. Underneath the sign were stairs that went down into the basement. The underground-hideout sort of vibe made Isshiki's eyes sparkle. "Knowing about good spots scores lots of points, you know!" Tugging at my sleeve, she clearly had high hopes.

So we arrived at one of the biggest Chiba ramen shops: Naritake. It's currently expanded not only to Tokyo, but also Nagoya. By the way, they've also opened a branch in Paris, France, where it's called Paritake (by me).

"...Agh, ramen?" As Isshiki gazed into the restaurant through the glass, her excitement visibly diminished. After all her tugging, she dropped my sleeve, too, and was now just standing there.

"Uh, I mean you said what I always have..."

"Agh, well, should have expected that from you," she said as if resigned, letting out a big sigh.

O-okay... It's true it's nothing fancy, but I didn't think this was something to be that disappointed about...

Based on my experience, I'd assumed girls liked ramen, too. Source: Miss Hiratsuka. Whoa, that's a real unreliable source. For starters, it would be crazy to count her as a "girl." How is it crazy, you ask? It just is.

Miss Hiratsuka would be ready and willing to have Naritake, if it would only nari-take her. But then conversely, as far as I knew, only Miss Hiratsuka would be like that.

To look at it another way here, this was a chance to get Isshiki into Naritake. As ancient generations once said: "A crisis is a crisis, and an opportunity is also a crisis." A crisis is only a crisis, and just when you *think* it's an opportunity, the rug is ready to get pulled out from under you. You have to stay sharp!

"If I could suggest you try it before making a judgment…" I suddenly started speaking deferentially to her without even thinking, trepidation coloring my voice.

Isshiki gave me a dead-eyed look but then nodded in resignation. "I was the one who said I'd leave it to you, so it's fine…"

Really? Really? It would be nice if that would convince her…

I had gained Isshiki's assent, reluctant though it was, and we went into the restaurant. Inside, someone energetically called out, "Hiya, 'elcome!"

Since it was lunchtime, the counter was mostly full, but fortunately, there were two seats open. I decided to go straight to the ticket machine to buy meal tickets. Isshiki's gaze wandered over the buttons as she looked at all the lines of characters. It seemed she had trouble deciding.

"My recommendation is the shoyu ramen," I said. "The miso is also good, but for your first time, it's good to start with the basics, right?"

"All right."

I bought a ticket for Isshiki and went to the counter. After I took a seat, the first thing out of my mouth was to say to the staff, "Extra."

"Extra? What?" Isshiki, who sat down next to me, gave me a questioning look.

"The amount of fat. Oh, and go easy on hers."

Naritake sold itself on back fat and strong flavors, so even if you ordered a regular, its flavor was more full-bodied compared with other ramen shops. I recommend a beginner start with the light.

"…You're used to this."

"I guess," I replied with a little pride, assuming she was showing appreciation that I was a regular. But then no reaction followed.

Glancing over, I saw she was leaning slightly away from me, giving me a dull look.

Hmm, it seems Irohasu was not saying that out of admiration… We're side-by-side at the counter, so whyever does she feel so distant…?

Hey, boys! Listen up! Boys speak proudly of their knowledge of "fancier" junk food like ramen and curry, but that apparently won't charm girls! Watch out if you think that makes you seem cooler!

Isshiki and I didn't particularly converse as we waited, so I was zoning out while looking at the kitchen ahead of me. "…The 'elcome guy is here today. We're lucky."

"Huh? What are you talking about?"

"Well, Naritake is generally good, but there's some individuality in the flavor, and it comes out different depending on the chef and their shifts. So my favorite is the guy who greets customers with a *Hiya, 'elcome.*"

"…Um, being knowledgeable isn't always a good thing," Isshiki said wearily, and that was right when the ramen arrived.

The extra-fatty ramen was like the peak of Mount Fuji, gleaming under the lights, the rising steam warming the hearts of all who beheld it.

"Whoa, the heck? Is this for real?" Seeing the bowl, Isshiki cried out in shock.

Now was not the time to be paying attention to her. "Time to eat." Following those solemn words, with chopsticks and ceramic spoon in hand, I ate, slurped, devoured, and drank it down. Its flavor was addictive.

Meanwhile, Isshiki seemed mildly put off as she watched me devote myself entirely to eating, but then she resolved herself with a little gulp and timidly picked up her chopsticks. She neatly brought her ceramic spoon to her mouth and closed her lips around it, and then her throat bobbed a little.

She froze. She was still like that for the briefest moment, but soon after, as if remembering herself, she roped in her noodles with her chopsticks and pursed her glossy lips, blew on her food, then began to eat carefully.

It seemed her impression was not a negative one. A little relieved by her reaction, I resumed my meal as well.

Neither of us said anything as we continued, and we were done eating before you knew it.

"...It's frustrating to admit...," she muttered. When I gave her a sidelong glance, Isshiki lifted her head and looked at me. Her expression seemed somehow vexed. She pouted her lips as she continued. "It was good...," she confessed, then immediately jerked her face away.

A smile broke on my lips. "...Good to hear it."

"Well, it might just score pretty high to get someone to take you to a restaurant that's hard to go to with other girls." Isshiki nodded to herself, and whoever she was trying to tell that to, she apparently convinced them all on her own.

I'm pleased to hear my selection was to your satisfaction.

Well, if you really thought about it, pasta and ramen were similar things, and in the sense of oil content, there's not much difference between avocado and back fat, either.

Carbs are just the greatest, irrespective of gender.

Naritake really is god tier.

$$\times \quad \times \quad \times$$

Guess it was time to go home, now that the meal was over!

...I would have said that out loud, but we were yet again trudging around Chiba city.

"Don't you want to eat something sweet?" Isshiki said, making her next order sound like a question, and so now we were wandering in search of some kind of café.

"Around *there*, you knooow, there's a place that seems pretty good!"

she said, striding briskly on ahead. She went to a spot a little ways from the central downtown hub, a street with a calm atmosphere lined with a park, offices, and apartment buildings.

Passing in front of Chuo Station, we walked down a clean road that had been repaved relatively recently. Unlike on the more chaotic Nanpa Street, the buildings were neat.

Perhaps that was the reason the wind blowing through felt a little stronger.

The north wind was still cold, despite the sun.

The ramen had left both my stomach and heart in a warm and comfortable state, so it wasn't like I was dying to go home right that minute. Still, I wasn't very keen on a long march, either.

When I turned to Isshiki to ask if this would take any longer, she pointed ahead with a bright smile.

"There. That one."

Glancing in the direction she was pointing, I saw a rather chic-looking café.

With its wood-paneled exterior, broad windows to let in natural light, big parasol on the terrace, and a menu written in chalk on the blackboard that sat on the frontage, it was the definition of fancy-schmancy. *Come on, is this for real? This is Chiba. Are we even allowed to have fancy cafés?*

How about it? This is fine, right? We're going in, right? It wouldn't make sense not to go, right? Isshiki was saying without words as she tugged on my scarf.

Listen, this isn't a leash, okay? "Well, this'll work, I guess."

I mean, it was cold, and anywhere was fine by me. This was the kind of place I'd never go if I'd been alone, but since Isshiki was with me that day, I'd probably be forgiven for darkening their doorstep.

"Okay then, let's g... Ohhh, shoot." Isshiki froze on the spot.

"What? What is it?"

With a yank on my sleeve, she brought me to a stop. *Uhhh, these aren't reins…*

Looking panicked, she circled behind me. Sneakily poking her head out from behind my back, she pointed at the storefront. "Look over there."

"Hmm?"

When I did as instructed, a couple came out of the café: a slightly timid-looking girl with braided pigtails and glasses, and a normal boy you'd see anywhere, with no particularly special characteristics… The two of them left the shop, then kept walking in the opposite direction from us.

"Huh." Watching them go, arms folded, I considered. *Hmm…I've seen them somewhere before… Who were they, again?*

A murmur came from behind me. "That's the vice president and the secretary."

…Ohhh, yeah. I should know them.

Hey, wait. Why were the two of them coming out of that café together?

"What, are those two dating?" I asked Isshiki.

Hopping away from my back, she cocked her head. "I dunno? I don't think so? I mean, assuming they're dating just because they're hanging out is a little close-mi—" Isshiki froze, then violently whipped back toward me. "Ah! Wait, were you just hitting on me? It's pretty shameless to act like you're my boyfriend when we've just hung out once so could you wait until we've at least gone out a bunch of times. I'm sorry." She shoved her hands out in front of her as if putting distance between us, then said that all in a rush. She rattled it off so fast, when she was done, she had to take a deep breath.

"…Yeah, sure, whatever you want." *I don't even want to bother asking why she's interpreting it like that…* It was getting ridiculous, counting the total number of times she had rejected me…

"Let's just go in. It's cold outside," I said to her, heading into the shop, and she pattered after me.

"Ah, wait uuup!"

Being that this was a classier brand of café, it was pretty nice on the inside, too. The tables and chairs seemed to have been carefully selected, and each set had a different style. The walls and the shelving were decorated with cute ornaments—it was the sort of interior that seemed like it would win over women.

We were shown to the right side from the entrance, with sofa seating that was fairly standard, compared with the other stuff in here. The light of the sun poured in from the street-facing window.

Isshiki, seated opposite me, immediately opened her menu. "Aghhh, man. It's so hard to decide, huh?" Despite the interrogative intonation, it seemed she didn't particularly expect a response from me, as she flipped through the menu at her own convenience

Emphasizing a love for sweets to play up her girlish act—impressively cunning, Irohasu. Very impressive. But, well, I'm sure there are plenty of girls who just like sweets, not as a ploy. There's a cookie monster in the clubroom who's always eating snacks, after all… Though lately she's also been eating a lot of crackers and stuff, too.

As Isshiki waffled over her choices, I zoned out watching her, and when she noticed my gaze, she spun the menu around to me.

Huhhh, they've got a lot of stuff… Macarons and roll cake, cheesecake, crème brûlée…and gelato and sorbet, eh? What *is* the difference between gelato and sorbet? Is this like asking about different members of the Shoufukutei *rakugo* school?

As I was thinking these trivial thoughts, comparing the text with the photos, Isshiki's head jerked up from her menu. "I've made up my mind."

"Okay. Then I'll call the server."

When I did, Isshiki pointed to her menu and ordered, "Assam tea and the macaron sandwich, please."

"And your house blend…and gelato."

Once we placed our orders, it was peaceful for a few moments.

The faint bossa nova–style background music, the warm air of the café, and the soft sunlight of the early afternoon created a unique atmosphere. The voices of the other customers were somehow distant and muffled, like sounds filtering through underwater.

That drew my attention just that much more to the person before me.

Isshiki seemed used to coming to this place, incredibly relaxed as she sank deep into the sofa. Leaning her cheek on her hand, elbow on the armrest, she turned her face to the window. She must have been looking forward to the macaron sandwich, as she was humming softly.

While listening to her quiet song, I gazed at the scenery out the window. Outside was the familiar city of Chiba, but seen through the single pane of glass of this stylish café, it seemed more dreamy than usual. Perhaps a café has the magic to give you these delusions.

Or did Isshiki come here because that was what she liked about it? Though she wasn't the only customer come to visit.

"Do you come here with the student council?" I asked, remembering the pair we had just seen, and Isshiki's head jerked toward me. She shook her head.

Then she suddenly clapped and put a hand to her chin as she considered a moment. "Ohhh, you mean the vice president and the secretary? *Mayyybe* this place did come up in conversation last week."

"Huhhh." *So then we just happened to run into each other, huh?*

Or maybe Mr. Vice President had taken this opportunity to ask Miss Secretary out, saying something like, *Why don't we check out that café Isshiki was talking about?* Eugh, cringe!! What the heck are they doing in that student council room? Stop screwing around and work.

…No, wait. Maybe it wasn't the vice president making the invitation. If that timid-looking secretary mustered up her courage to ask him out, then that would kind of make me want to cheer her on! Though it doesn't particularly make me want to root for him! I feel like in my head, the vice president went into the same category as Tobe. In the sense that he's yet another victim of Iroha Isshiki.

As I pondered these matters, the perpetrator in question, Iroha Isshiki, was continuing to talk. "So, like, I was asking the vice president things like where do you hang out on weekends and stuff. For today. For today!" she said, as if emphasizing that last part, and then looked up through her lashes at me.

Did she just say that twice because it was important? This girl… That sort of blatant call to attention is not worth a lot of points, in Hachiman terms.

"I appreciate the sentiment, but I'd rather you prepared in more fundamental areas…" *You know, like asking if I want to go first, or actually explaining to me why you wanted to hang out at all. There were lots of things you should have done…*

It seemed Isshiki meant to ignore my complaints, blatantly averting her eyes as she hemmed and hawed under her breath, changing the subject. "Well, I honestly wasn't expecting to nearly bump into them here…"

She trailed off, then brought her gaze to the front again, fixing her eyes straight on me. And then—as if she didn't want anyone around to hear—she cupped a hand by her mouth with a bashful smile and whispered conspiratorially. "Next time, let's pick some place where there aren't so many people we know."

"Is there gonna be a next time…?"

My voice had gone dry from surprise and imagining this "next time" that would be brutal.

Isshiki glared at me. "Why are you acting so reluctant?"

"It's not like I don't want to go… Well, um, you know, I'll be sure to take appropriate measures to ensure the matter is dealt with."

"From that answer, it doesn't feel like it'll actually ever happen…"

Isshiki sighed, then looked at me with a slight twist of a smile, exasperated. "Oh!" she exclaimed with a sparkle of excitement in her eyes. When I turned around to see where she was looking—in other words, behind me—right at that moment, the server was bringing over her macaron sandwich and tea.

Her order, followed by my gelato and coffee, was placed neatly on the table. Isshiki watched it ecstatically before pulling out her phone and beginning to snap photos. For some reason, she was even taking shots of my gelato, not just her own cake.

Why is it that girls take pictures of food? Is it a food diary thing? Or is some trainer at a RIZAP gym telling them to send photos of their meals?

Satisfied with her pictures, Isshiki put down her phone. *Now we can finally eat*, I thought.

Isshiki's hand shot up. "Oh! Pardooon! Can I ask you to take a picture?" she called, and a server popped up and respectfully accepted the phone from Isshiki.

More pictures? Just how long is she going to make me wait?! I'm eating my ice cream! I thought, picking up my spoon, when she smacked my hand down.

Looking over, I saw her leaning slightly forward over the table, making a perfect posed expression toward the server holding up the phone. "Come on! Give me a peace sign!"

"No. You don't need me in your picture. And my ice cream is gonna melt."

"It won't melt that fast. C'mon, hurry," Isshiki retorted quickly without turning toward me. It seemed she couldn't maintain that pose for very long. Her cutesy mask was slipping a little, too.

"Um, sir…" The server was giving me this uncomfortable smile as if trying to see what to do. It made me feel not only uncomfortable, but pressured, too.

S-sorry for bothering you while you're working...

"Come *on*. Come on."

With Isshiki urging me, I had no choice but to slide my plate off to the side and lean over the table.

"If you could go a little closer in...," instructed the server, holding the camera, and I leaned forward a bit more.

Suddenly, I could smell shampoo. Sliding my eyes in that direction, I saw Isshiki's soft-looking hair flowing down. Her face was shockingly close. Just as I was about to automatically jerk back, the server called, "Oh yes, that's good. Say cheese!"

Then I heard the sound of a shutter click two, three times.

"Thank you sooo much!" Isshiki called out to the server.

Sinking deep into the sofa, I watched her accept the phone from the server. *I never thought taking a photo could be so exhausting...* Maybe there was some truth in the old saying that having your photo taken will steal your soul.

My sigh made the steam rising from my coffee cup vanish. I wanted to drink it before it got cold. "...Can I eat now?"

"Oh, yes. Go ahead," Isshiki replied casually as she checked over the photos.

Aw man, I bet my face was all red, I thought. To cool my head, I went for the ice cream that I'd been forced to wait on.

...I knew it would melt.

×   ×   ×

By the time I paid for the food and left the café, it was already dark out. It seemed quite some time had passed as we sat there engaging in trivial conversation and enjoying the food.

A bit of a breeze had come with nightfall, and the chilly air was coming in through the gaps of my loosely wrapped scarf, making me shiver. When I tugged together the collar of my coat and tightened my scarf, Isshiki emerged from the café after me.

"Sorry to make you wait. I almost forgot to take the receipt." She bopped herself on the head bashfully and stuck her tongue out, and I could almost hear her giggle, *Tee-hee.* ☆

She knew what she was doing…

Why would she even need that receipt? I just paid for the both of us. And hey, she took the receipts from the Ping-Pong place and the food ticket from the ramen shop, too, huh…? Is she going to file them on her tax return or something?

"All right, then let's just head for the station," I said.

"Okay," she replied, and when I nodded back at her, we started off, neither of us particularly leading the way.

Some people were headed toward the station, while others were just coming from it. The flow of traffic clashed, and the face of the city transformed to nighttime. It was the weekend, so the streets were busy.

It wasn't that late, but a yawn slipped out of me anyway, maybe because of the Ping-Pong. It seemed the same was true for Isshiki, walking along the sidewalk beside me, and she caught my infectious yawn.

When she realized I'd seen her, she looked a little self-conscious. Then, clearing her throat as if to cover it, she came a half step closer to me. "Wellll, I guess I'll give you ten points for today," she declared out of the blue. It seemed this was my grade for that day's Date Course Investigation Exam.

"Just out of curiosity, ten points out of what?"

"A hundred, duh."

"Why's my score so low…?"

I was trying, in my own way. Come on. Don't you think that's a little harsh? I complained with my eyes.

She began counting her fingers on her gloved hands. "Ummm… First of all, minus ten points for not being Hayama."

"You're asking the impossible right off the bat."

What the heck? Who does she think she is? Princess Kaguya? And she's grading me by subtracting points. Hachiman thinks adding points just might be better in order to encourage growth. Let's develop our strengths!

Obviously, she couldn't hear the screams of my heart. She lowered another finger on her left hand, and then another as she counted off. *Please stop. Your fingers are lowering for now, but my heart will sink forever...*

"And then minus forty points for your behavior in general?"

"Well, that's fair." I nodded automatically. In fact, I must have put in some real effort, if that was all that got deducted. Rather than me putting in a good effort, I should say that Isshiki had been the one making an effort here, in having forgiven it.

"At least you're self-aware..." She sighed, her voice tinged with resignation.

Oh, so she hasn't actually forgiven me, huh...?

Professor Isshiki's scoring continued. Suddenly squeezing her right hand in a fist, she sent it straight into a light punch in my side. "And minus fifty points for being so eager to hang out with a girl when she invited you."

"*You're* the one who invited *me*... And wait, now it's zero." It didn't hurt where she punched me, but mysteriously, I did feel a little stab to the heart. I just happened to remember someone that moment, and it weirdly stuck in my head.

As I rubbed my ribs, Isshiki hopped ahead one step, stuck up a finger, and puffed out her chest. "But I had fun, so I'll give you an extra ten points."

"...Well, thanks."

So that gave me the total of ten points, huh? She was merciless with her scoring, but the last part was a little sweet. I would have given myself the same score.

We gradually drew near the station as we talked.

I was going on to the Sobu Line, while Isshiki would probably head home by monorail. So then we'd be parting ways here, in front of the station.

"How was it for you?" Isshiki asked me hesitantly as we approached the short staircase that lead to the roundabout. Her face was slightly downturned, so I couldn't see her expression, and I couldn't tell at a glance what she was asking about.

I doubted it was too different from what I'd been thinking about just now.

"Well, basically what you said... Though I'm a little tired."

"Did you need to be that honest? ...Whatever. It just means you put all your energy into having fun with me!" She lifted her head, a cutesy smile on her face. I couldn't help but make a face at her customary slyness.

Seeing my reaction, Isshiki pouted. "Why are you acting like I'm a high-maintenance pain in the butt or something...?" She puffed up her cheeks, then pointed her nose in the air and strode off a little on the fast side. As she passed by me, she said in a sulky tone, "*All* girls are high-maintenance, you know."

That made sense to me. With a little shrug, I hurried to catch up to her. "...Yeah, I'm sure. Everyone on the planet is annoying."

"Including you! Geez!" Spinning around, Isshiki was giving me such a beleaguered look, it didn't even compare to the one I'd given her just now. Ouch.

Perhaps our mutual beleaguered feelings slowed our pace a little. Regardless, the station concourse was just ahead. Threading through the throngs of people emerging from the turnstile, we arrived right in front of the same ad screens where we'd met up that day. Isshiki stopped. I halted in my tracks.

"Anyway, today has been educational. Thank you very much." She thanked me with surprising honesty, then slowly bowed.

I was taken aback by the utter sincerity and politeness, and when I muttered something flustered like *Uh-huh* or *Mm* or *No, thank you*, she lifted her head and giggled like she found me funny. "…You be sure to put our research to good use, too, okay?"

Her gaze was overflowing with kindness, but there was just a bit of severity behind her words.

"…Sure. Well, uh, thanks for today, then."

It was true that I'd learned a lot—through no fault of my own, though. Isshiki was a unique person, but I highly doubted my experience would be directly useful for anyone else. Because everyone is a special case for someone, and everyone is different.

"See you at school, then," she said.

"Get home safe."

We exchanged farewells, and then Isshiki headed to the stairs for the monorail platform. The escalator slowly rose, and she gradually drew away.

Suddenly, she spun back around to give me a little wave. I raised a casual hand in response, watching her as she grew distant.

Girls are made of sugar and spice and everything nice.

Iroha Isshiki's version of nice is sweet and spicy. And probably bitter and sour, too. And a real hassle, something you won't know until you try coming into contact with it.

I'm sure it's not unique to Isshiki—the other girls in my life would have it, too.

What is it, exactly?

Watching Iroha Isshiki go until she was out of sight, I wondered that, just a bit.

Ｚｚｚ

There lies **the deadline** they absolutely cannot fail to make.

The clubroom seemed colder than normal.

Since we'd told Miss Hiratsuka about the clunking heater, we'd been asked to refrain from using it until the repair technician came to fix it.

The clubroom was unoccupied during the day, so this had minimal effect on our lives, but it was a different story after school. We needed to perform our duties as the sun was slowly setting, and the temperature was dropping. This meant that despite being indoors, I had my scarf tight around my neck. The only other heating device in the room was the electric kettle.

Except that wasn't its intended use. As always, the electric kettle was being used purely for boiling tea. But its humidifying effect helped; little wisps of steam were better than nothing.

It's hard for humans to adjust to losing a comfortable lifestyle and go into "starvation mode." Whenever I felt the cold air radiate off the floor, my hand would stop moving instead of turning a page in my paperback.

The club hardly got any visitors anyway. If I was just going to be killing time, I'd say my house was definitively more comfortable. I could even go to Starbucks or something, even if I felt a little out of place, and it might be better to read while surrounded by pretentious types (lol). Anyway, why is it that those pretentious types (lol) at Starbucks deliberately choose seats by the window to type away on their MacBooks and show off their new books? Do they want to be those bugs that stick to the window at night?

Well, it would be hard to read at the popular Starbucks. In that sense, the sparsely populated clubroom was superior. I wasn't averse to the quiet and cool atmosphere. But in the winter, the coolness really revved up a lot.

My spot was right by the wall adjoining the hallway. This wall was so thin, we could have been in a cheap hotel room. It would be more accurate to call this a panel. So it was not much to rely on when it came to keeping out the outside air, and drafts seeped in from the cracks between the sliding doors, too.

"…Hey, can we call it a day? I'm cold," I said to the two sitting by the window, shivering.

Once I became aware of it, I just couldn't take the cold anymore.

Yukinoshita looked up from her book and cocked her head. "Is it? …I suppose it is. What do you suggest we do about it?" She put her hand to her chin in a thinking pose.

"Really? I'm totally fine," Yuigahama responded.

Of course *she* wouldn't be cold.

As soon as Yuigahama had felt the slightest bit cold, she'd gleefully moved her chair to squish right next to Yukinoshita. They shared a blanket hanging over both their laps. Normally, Yukinoshita would complain about the heat or the annoyingness and move away, but she was letting Yuigahama do as she pleased for this day only.

The both of them were looking downright cozy.

Part of it was because they were sitting in a sunny spot, but the biggest factor was that they were sharing body heat.

You guys look so warm…

As I was gazing upon this happy pair, Yuigahama straightened up from her position leaning on Yukinoshita. "H-Hikki, is it cold over there?"

"…Yeah, well, it's cold, yeah." When she brought it to my attention, I felt the cold air creeping up on me to make me shiver. I found myself unconsciously rubbing my arms.

"Oh…" Yuigahama flipped up the blanket once, as if checking its size. And then with a moment's pause, as if feeling hesitant, she let out a little sigh.

She flicked a gaze over at me with questioning, puppy-dog eyes, which made me fidget.

Yuigahama took in a deep breath like she was going to say something, her full chest rising and falling with determination. Her meek voice didn't match her grand gestures. "I—I see…"

As she was hemming and hawing under her breath, Yukinoshita took over with a gentle smile. "Why not put on a jacket?"

I knew it. I grabbed my coat as she suggested and hung it casually over my shoulders without putting my arms through, like a woman suffering from the office air conditioner blasting in the summer.

Isn't it time to go home yet…? I wondered. I was having a staring contest with the clock hanging on the wall when there came a knocking on the door. *Agh, someone's here… Looks like I won't be able to go home early.*

"Come in," Yukinoshita called out, ignoring my dejected slumping. After Yukinoshita gave the go-ahead, the door opened.

"Hello, everyone!" When our visitor bobbed her head in a bow, her pale hair swayed. Large round eyes peeked out from under the gaps in her flowing bangs, and her lips formed a faint smile.

Iroha Isshiki had come to our clubroom yet again. But her greeting was rather more polite than usual, and it gave me the slightest hint that something was off. *I've kinda got a bad feeling about this…*

"Ohhh, Iroha-chan. Yahallooo!" Yuigahama raised a hand and called to her, and Isshiki waved back, the sleeves of her cardigan fluttering.

"Yeah, hellooo!" Returning her greeting, Isshiki strolled into the clubroom, then stopped suddenly. "…Is anyone else cold in here?" She gave Yukinoshita a questioning look.

Yukinoshita smiled, at a loss. "Yes, the heater is broken right now."

"Ohhh, really?" Isshiki said with disinterest, picking up a chair. She headed over to Yukinoshita, sat herself right down, tugged over the blanket, and joined their impromptu human *kotatsu*.

"H-hey…" Yukinoshita's tone was partly confused and partly accusatory as Isshiki suddenly pasted herself against her. Isshiki didn't seem to care. "Sooo waaarm! ♪" she said to herself as she snuggled in closer to the other girl.

"Ah, should we pack it in more?" Yuigahama suggested gently.

"Ohhh, thanks sooo much!" Isshiki sounded like a spoiled child. Now Yukinoshita was being squeezed from both sides.

Stop it! Don't press Yukinon any more! She's already flat to begin with! A wind blows over her Kanto Chest Plains! If you're going to press her, at least push up!

I never would have said that out loud. As I was worrying about whether I should put a stop to the Isshiki/Yuigahama sandwich, the squishing continued.

"…Agh." Yukinoshita sighed in resignation, then drew her chair back slightly, opening up a space so that it was easier for Isshiki to get in.

Isshiki gleefully exclaimed, "Yaaay!" She moved her chair over in little scooches, somehow getting even closer to Yukinoshita.

Yukinoshita gave Isshiki an annoyed look, but her hands did not say the same, as she reached out to the quilted teapot cover and began pouring tea into a paper cup. "…Would you like some tea?"

"Th-thank you very much." Isshiki accepted the steaming cup, and holding it in both hands to keep them warm, she began to sip.

They look so warm...

But anyway, Yuigahama isn't the only one getting special treatment. You've also gotten softer on Isshiki lately, too, hmm, Miss Yukinoshita...?

Now that I was thinking about it, though, for Yukinoshita, they would be her first real friend and real junior. It was kind of charming to see her take on a bit of a caretaking role.

As I watched the three warm-looking girls from my chilly spot far away, Isshiki, seeming quite comfy as she drank her hot tea, gave me a little bow. "Oh, thanks for the other day."

"Hmm, yeah," I replied noncommittally.

Yukinoshita and Yuigahama looked over at me, wondering what we were talking about.

Urk, it's kind of hard to explain...

The two of us had just gone to hang out together. That was all it was, but if I went out of my way to tell Yukinoshita and Yuigahama, *We just hung out; it was nothing*, it would seem like more than just "nothing."

But remaining silent brought about its own weird feeling of guilt. *Well, I guess I've already made it a big deal by feeling guilty in the first place, huh...? Ewww, Hachiman is such a creep...*

As a result, all I could do was let out a meaningless exhalation, a combination of a sigh and a moan. This must have appeared suspicious, as Yukinoshita's eyebrows came together, while Yuigahama glanced between Isshiki and me.

Oh dear...

For a while, the clubroom fell into an awkward silence. Despite the cold, I could feel the sweat glands on my head gradually opening up.

Isshiki cleared her throat softly, breaking the tension. "Sooo I've kinda been thinking...maybe the student council should make a free magazine," she announced, making a remark completely unconnected to our earlier comments.

Yukinoshita gave her a questioning look. "Hmm? A free magazine?"

Nice one, Irohasu! I've been liberated from their scrutiny...

"A free magazine is, like, one of those, right?" asked Yuigahama.

"Yeah, one of those," Isshiki replied, completing a brief exchange in which no information was communicated whatsoever.

The other day, when Zaimokuza came to the clubroom, I did recall the discussion touching on free magazines, so it seemed even a few, brief comments like that was enough to get it across.

What was not getting across was her goal.

"But why a free magazine?" Yukinoshita asked with a tilt of her head.

Isshiki drew one hand out from under the blanket and waved a finger as she explained, "We report our accounts at the end of the fiscal year! So the vice president and the rest of student council have put together the paperwork for that, but apparently this year, we actually have some budget left over."

"Ohhh...," I said. The previous student council president had been Meguri. Megu☆rin was so fluffy, I didn't really get the impression she was very tightfisted when it came to money matters. It kinda made sense to me that she'd leave leftover funds.

But Iroha Isshiki—Iro☆hasu—the current student council president, was so shrewd that I was sure she'd be having an eye on the money...

As I was mulling over the matter, just as expected, Isshiki smacked her hands in front of her chest and grinned brightly. "Since we've got the money, wouldn't it be best to use it? It seems like a free magazine would be just right."

"That doesn't mean you need to make us do extra work..."

That makes no sense. No matter how much money you have left over, creating work for yourself is simply a mystery... This girl is definitely plotting something..., I thought, giving her a suspicious look. Isshiki just gave a cutesy "Aha!" to skirt the issue. *Th-that's even more suspicious...*

"But then, Iroha-chan. If you have extra, wouldn't it be best to save it up? Saving is important, you know?" Yuigahama chided. *Sounds like something a mom would say...*

But if this were Isshiki's own money, she'd be right. The difference here was the fact that this was the student council budget.

Yukinoshita, who had been listening to them talk, must also have realized this, and she put her hand to her chin. "I'm sure they can't."

"Why not?" Yuigahama asked, leaning her head on Yukinoshita's shoulder.

"Since if they have budget left over, they might have their budget cut next year. If I were in charge of determining their budget, that's what I would do," Yukinoshita explained.

"Yes! That's exactly it! Sooo wouldn't it just be better to splurge before the end of year, to keep my budget from getting cut next year?" Isshiki inched in real close, then leaned up against Yukinoshita cutely in an attempt to win her over.

"Too close..." The answer was feeble and filled with confusion.

Sandwiched from both sides, Yukinoshita was cramped like an unfortunate passenger on the train at rush hour. Mm-hmm, such good friends!

But, well, it's not like I didn't know where Isshiki was coming from. Though it wasn't actually Isshiki's money. *What the heck is she saying, "my budget"...? It's the student council's.* But if it would fit in that budget, then the printing of a free magazine itself wouldn't really be a problem.

"Seems fine to me. Though I dunno what kind you're making," I said with little interest.

Moving away from Yukinoshita, Isshiki turned back to me. "About thaaat, we've basically already decided. I was thinking it'd be nice if we could feature, like, places to hang *out*, or good *restaurants*, or cute *cafés*."

"Ohhh, that sounds nice! And it might be cool to add in clothing stores, or those shops with the little household items, too!" Yuigahama got all excited about Isshiki's idea, squishing even closer to Yukinoshita.

Yukinoshita was really suffering now. "So you're imagining something like a mini community bulletin, or a community magazine. It seems like there would be a demand, content-wise…"

But places to hang out, good food, and cute cafés, huh…? I feel like that rang a few bells. What was it, "People are nice"? *Places to hang ooout and good fooood and cute cafés are waiting*, right? The only part that fits is the food, huh? Guess I'm wrong.

"If we're talking community magazines, then would it be kinda like *Chiba Walker*?" Yuigahama asked, turning her body toward Isshiki.

"Yep, yep." Isshiki nodded, leaning forward enthusiastically. Finally freed from the other girls, Yukinoshita let out a short sigh.

Isshiki continued her explanation. "If it spreads information, we can just go out to have fun and call it research while we guzzle down the bankroll."

With that cutesy ☆ cute smile of hers on, she was endorsing something close to embezzlement. *Guzzle down funds…? This isn't a developer's comment about extorting microtransactions in a gacha game…*

Yukinoshita and I were both utterly disturbed, but Yuigahama was tilting her head.

"Bankroll…"

I can just see her imagining cake… It's not a Swiss roll.

Isshiki must have seen from our faces—Yuigahama aside—that we were completely put off, and she puffed up her cheeks in a pout. "Ohhh, you told me before, didn't you? *Like, if it's getting bankrolled anyway, then use it how you like!*" she said.

Yukinoshita shot me a cold look. "I see you've been teaching her nothing good…"

"Wait, I didn't say that," I argued back.

Isshiki shook her head, giving me a sulking, grumpy look. "You did! You definitely said it when we were planning the Christmas event."

Did I say that back then…? Something about how it was a joint event with another school, so not to worry about the money and use it all up… I did, yeah. Give this girl an inch, and she'd take a mile. Except she'd completely twisted what I said…

"People could take what you're trying to do as appropriating student council funds for personal use…," Yukinoshita said, her manner accusatory.

Isshiki replied, quite indifferently, "Buuut this could be a good opportunity for everyone at school to learn about these things, and we can enjoy ourselves, too, sooo isn't it win-win?"

My! That Tamanawa boy has been such a bad influence… Your father won't let you spend time with a boy like that!

"When you put it like that, it doesn't feel like a bad thing…" Yuigahama said thoughtfully.

It was hard to make a sweeping claim that this was wrong, if having fun was to the benefit of everyone else. It was like commodifying your hobby. Ideal, really.

I got that Isshiki's proposal was not unreasonable. What remained was the issue of whether this was realistic.

Yukinoshita folded her arms, considering this for a moment. "But then will your application for the funds actually go through?"

"Aw, Yukinoshita! Making sure it goes through is the treasurer's job!" Isshiki answered, giggling like she found this absolutely hilarious.

She's a hot mess… Well, if anything happens, she's the one taking responsibility, so it's fine, I guess.

If the treasurer was responsible for the expense report going through, then it was the duty of the responsible party to get thrown under the bus! Taking responsibility was their responsibility!

Who knows if Isshiki was aware of this, but it seemed she had more than enough enthusiasm to make up for any deficits. "Sooo then the only issue is the free magazine… How should we make it?" she asked, starting up this new topic like this was the reason she'd come.

Hmm, enthusiasm is the one thing she has in spades…

"I dunno… It's not like we've ever made a free magazine…," I said.

"Yes…it's fair to say we know nothing on the matter," Yukinoshita agreed.

Listening from the side, Yuigahama clapped her hands as if remembering something. "Oh, but before, we did that page in that community magazine."

"Oh, now that you mention it, we did…" I think that was the thing Miss Hiratsuka had brought to us. She'd been saddled with making one to revitalize local businesses or something, so she'd gotten us to do a spread on weddings aimed at the younger generation. It had been a real struggle.

Thinking back on that, we were discussing it a bit when Isshiki suddenly leaned forward. "That sounds like a great idea! I get the feeling it'll work!"

"With that, we just needed to fill up one extra page. Creating something from scratch is an entirely different situation. It's impossible," Yukinoshita chided.

Isshiki dejectedly sat back down again, shoulders slumping as she gazed up at Yukinoshita. "…Is it really?"

"It is really," Yukinoshita said coldly.

When Isshiki sniffled, looking resentful like a begging child, even Yukinoshita was speechless, quietly glancing away.

Oh no! At this rate, Yukinoshita is definitely going to give in!

Yukinoshita could be brutally objective when it came to logic and words, but when pressured by emotions and gestures, she gave in with surprising ease. Source: her usual exchanges with Yuigahama.

With Isshiki's innocent eyes on her, Yukinoshita twisted around uncomfortably.

Yuigahama cut in. "Hey now, couldn't you just do a little research on how to make one of these things? And ask people who might know some stuff and get them to help… Then we'd be able to do it with you!"

Isshiki grinned. "You're so nice, Yui!"

But if you really scrutinized her words, she was implying to "come back when you're actually ready," disguised in a gentle way.

As expected of Yuigahama. She knew how to suck up to Yuki-noshita, which meant Isshiki's pleas were not effective on her.

"Well, Yuigahama's right," I said. "If you really want to do it, then you should take some time to prepare."

With all three of us criticizing her, Isshiki's expression became troubled, her eyebrows in an upside-down V. "I can't."

"Why not?" I asked.

She looked down before muttering solemnly, "…Because it's almost time for the closing of accounts."

I got the feeling we'd just heard some very heavy words.

Oh yeah, it's right before the end of the fiscal year, huh? My parents seem busier than usual, too. It seems that around this time of year, all the corporate cogs out there had a lot to do.

According to the Internet, which is always right, the reason in February and March you get merch like Blu-ray box sets or OVAs coming out all at the same time is because it's near the end of the fiscal year.

Well, this isn't limited purely to anime-related things. It's common enough to shove out product around this time of year to bump up the annual sales and balance the accounts. Source: my mom and dad. They were working frantically that day, like every day…

"I didn't really understand all the details myself, *buuut* it looks like if we're gonna shove it into this fiscal year, we have to do it before the expense report at the beginning of March, and we're already past the beginning of February, so right now is our only opportunity!" Isshiki said in a rush, waving her hands as she explained quite earnestly. Her gestures were very cute, but hearing her say terms like *fiscal* and *expense report* and *shove* was not…

Well, I understood there wasn't much time. They'd assemble all their receipts and invoices within the month, then process them at the beginning of the following month.

Which means we have to finish the job this month, huh…?

Though we weren't far into February, it was a short month. And even if it was just a free magazine, starting up a whole magazine from scratch was a monumentally difficult task.

"Totally impossible. Give it up," I said. Yukinoshita quietly nodded, and Yuigahama got this awkward strained smile.

You can lean forward and look up at me with those wibbly eyes, but it's no use. What's impossible is impossible. I slowly shook my head.

Isshiki quietly stood. "Hey…there's something I have to talk about…," she said in a lowered voice before softly walking over and stopping in front of my seat. She kept her face turned away as if she felt hesitant.

"Talk about what…?" I asked, but Isshiki just wouldn't say it. Yukinoshita and Yuigahama were both giving her questioning looks.

Isshiki ignored our confusion, and then for some reason, she undid one button of her blazer, then another. *Wait. What the heck is she doing?*

I wasn't the only one shocked—Yukinoshita's and Yuigahama's mouths were hanging open, too. *Hey, wait, seriously, what is she doing?! Oh man, hey, um, you're not gonna strip, right?! Do you know how much trouble that would cause for me?*

As Isshiki twisted around to pull off her blazer, she gave a little grunt of effort. Then she reached under her pink cardigan with one hand and began rummaging around in the chest of her blouse.

"Um…" She sounded unsure as she fished around in there. With each movement, her loosely open collar revealed flashes of her collarbone. Feeling like I shouldn't be looking at point-blank range, I averted my eyes, but that just made the sound of rustling clothes and her breathing seem more suggestive.

"I don't know what you're doing, but do it far away from me. Go." With my face turned down, I shooed her away with my hand, leaning away as much as I could.

Isshiki let out a particularly big sigh. "Ah, here it is," she announced, and with another rustle, she pulled out some paper. Her other hand gently took mine, and then she pressed the paper into my palms.

The sudden touch of her hand, the feel of her thin, supple fingers, and her mysteriously soft skin made me freeze up in surprise, and she jerked her hand away. Left in my grip were the warm pieces of paper.

When I realized that warmth was from her body heat, it just about made my hand ooze with sweat. I timidly opened my clenched fist.

There were a few of those pieces of paper. Skimming over them, I saw rows of familiar characters. Printed at the top was *Receipt*, while underneath was written the name of a bowling alley and a café. There was even the food ticket for a ramen shop, too.

No way, these receipts…

With a gasp, I figured it out, and when I lifted my head, my eyes locked with Isshiki's. She was grinning.

You looked? You saw them, right? Then you get it now, right? her smile seemed to say, and with that before me, any explanation in words was unnecessary.

Isshiki put her hand out, prompting me to return the receipts. When I complied and handed them back, she took them carefully in both hands, then tucked them away again in the chest pocket of her blouse.

"Sooo about what I wanted to talk about…" She repeated what

she'd said before in a sweet, coaxing voice. It seemed she meant to imply that I was complicit here.

But I didn't think I had anything to do with this. I'd paid for myself, and it's not like I'd received any monetary benefit.

So then why do I feel so guilty…? It was fun, so then in the broadest sense, I benefited from her bankroll? No, but…well…

Maybe it was just because Isshiki had brought out those receipts with such confidence, but I became more and more worried that maybe I had done something bad. I could kind of understand why a victim might be pressured to confess to a false accusation…

I cleared my throat, then turned back to Isshiki. Time for a plea bargain!

"…L-let's just hear more about it, for now."

"Has she blackmailed you?!" Yuigahama cried out in shock.

"Agh…" Yukinoshita sighed in exasperation at the same time.

$$\times \quad \times \quad \times$$

Some time passed since Isshiki had headed back to the student council room to grab some papers so that she could talk to us about the details. While we awaited her return, Yukinoshita poured us more tea.

As the steam rose from our cups, the smell of black tea wafted through the room. The heater still wasn't working, but the tea and the jacket over my shoulders kept the cold from bothering me too much.

"Sorry for the waaait!" The door was flung open with a rattle, and Isshiki bounded into the room.

She dumped the file folders in her arms, then began spreading out on the desk what seemed to be the relevant materials. Her eyes sparkled with excitement and glee like a child looking at a flyer for a toy store right before Christmas.

Seeing her enthusiasm did make me want to make this free

magazine happen somehow, but this wasn't something that would just work out with enough enthusiasm, guts, and idealism.

First of all, we needed an accurate grasp of the situation. The more you understand the nature of the work, the more cornered you feel about your present situation.

If there's no wiggle room in cost or schedule, then it can't be actualized in the first place, and if you are fully aware of that and forced into an unrealistic plan anyway, that kills motivation. Conversely, when there's leeway in the budget and schedule, you think it'll be a cinch and end up with a train wreck from some careless mistake. *Awww man. In all the scenarios I'm envisioning, everything falls to shit as soon as the work is assigned…*

That is precisely why the correct route is to understand your capacity for work. In fact, it would be better to not accept responsibilities in the first place. Or, in the case where refusal isn't an option, you should negotiate to reduce as much of your workload as possible. Having been in the exploitative environment of the Service Club for the past year, I had finally become enlightened to this.

I called out to Isshiki while waiting for her to finish laying out all the papers. "Let me make this clear: We still haven't decided we're going to go through with this. We'll hear what specifically you plan to do, and based on that, we'll consider if we can do it or not."

"Right. I'm fine with that!" she answered cheerfully, beaming at me.

Ack…when you look at me with those hopeful eyes, it makes it really hard to say no…

While I was choked up, Yukinoshita took over, beginning the discussion so we could move things along. "All right, could you tell us about your printing plans?"

"Right. Ummm, *wellll*, I contacted the printing company that we placed an order with for the Christmas event and asked them some stuff." Isshiki grabbed a few papers from her collection. It seemed she had a pamphlet, plus a written quote.

Holy crap… She's already spoken to the printing firm? For someone who can't make plans, she's certainly proactive…

"They recommended this…" Isshiki pointed to one spot on the pamphlet.

Beside her, Yukinoshita examined it. "Eight pages full color… That's quite a bold move…" She pressed her temple as if she was starting to get a headache.

Isshiki had on a shy smile. "Ohhh, well, that was what we decided on! The conversation kinda just went in that direction!"

"What kind of conversation just 'goes in that direction'…?" I asked in exasperation.

Isshiki puffed up her cheeks. "I meeean, when an adult tells you something, you wind up going with it, right?"

"I get that. I understand where you're coming from…" Yuigahama nodded along in emphatic agreement.

Kids these days… I hope no adults or older kids try to take advantage of them.

"For the number of copies…well, we can just go off the budget… We can secure space within the school, if need be, and they can be recycled… It seems the risk of remaining inventory would not be a concern." Meanwhile, Yukinoshita wasn't listening to either of them, going over the materials at her own pace and muttering to herself.

Hmm, Discommunication Girl… I'm worried about you for other reasons!

After poring over the pamphlet, Yukinoshita looked up to push the papers over to me. I took them and flipped through them as well. They described the steps involved in a simple printing process.

"They'll handle the design and input the information for production… So all we have to do is draft the content and rough design," Yukinoshita explained.

"Hmm. Seems like it won't be any different from the community bulletin," I observed.

Basically, we'd be fine if we focused on getting the content done. However, we still had to prearrange the photos and article text. *Prearrange* is term that conveys a particularly excessive level of pretension.

"Though it's quite a few more pages than what we did before…," Yukinoshita replied, grim resolve in her voice.

Yuigahama seemed peppier than usual. "But, like, we've got the student council this time around, so if we all share the work, we can figure it out, right?"

"Oh, you're mostly right…," I began, when I caught sight of Isshiki quietly turning away with a sour look on her face.

"…"

"…Isshiki? Why are you so quiet?" Yukinoshita smiled brightly at her, voice tender and gaze warm. But strangely, I sensed no warmth there, and the sight made a shiver run down my spine.

Okay, that really skeeves me out…

It seemed Isshiki felt the same fear—no, she must have been even more rattled, as she flailed in a panic. "Ah! Oh, n-no! Um…everyone's a *little* busy right now with the end-of-year stuff, but once that's done, I think there should be no problem…"

"…In other words, you're saying we can't expect help this time." Yukinoshita let out a weak sigh.

Isshiki's shoulders slumped apologetically. "No…"

"C-come on, guys, there's nothing we can do about that. If you don't have enough help, maybe you could ask some friends to give you a hand… Let's just…do whatever we gotta do!" Yuigahama said encouragingly as she made a fist.

But when she says *whatever we gotta*, I think she more means just "let's do whatever"…

Anyway, we could see the labor cost and quantity. We'd gotten a grasp on the minimum number of personnel available. All that was left was to learn the schedule. Figure out that part, and we could decide if it was possible or not.

Isshiki had just told us the plan in rough and that it was within the month, but we had to pound out a more detailed schedule.

"So when do you have to get it done, exactly?" I asked her.

"Soon, real soon." Isshiki pulled out the schedule sheet and tapped it. "Right now, the budget will be *perfect* if we get the discount for the early plan. For that to happen, we have to hand over this…input info? Whatever. We need to give that to the printing company by mid-February."

Oh-ho, an early-bird discount. They have those? If she's making it with the remaining funds, then it should be no problem. And this looks like it'll make it just perfectly by the accounting deadline, too—that Irohasu knows how to manage her money! I thought, doing my best to escape reality, but even so, I couldn't ignore one phrase that had stuck with me.

When I was tilting my head thinking, *Hmm? By mid-February?* Isshiki added in a quiet mutter, "…So in, like…two more weeks."

"What? That's impossible. Two weeks is totally impossible," I answered instantly, flailing my hands in refusal.

Opposite me, Yukinoshita nodded slowly. "That's not correct. If we assume there will be an editorial check to confirm all content to be published and apply for revisions, then we should assume we have one week."

"Even less time?!" Yuigahama turned to Yukinoshita in shock.

"We're just talking about the best-case scenario if everything goes well… We're already behind schedule from the get-go… We should consider unforeseen situations and try to accelerate the process." Yukinoshita went on with her logical and dispassionate explanation until that point, but it seemed that once she'd said it herself, even she understood it was unrealistic.

"…Of course, this is only if we were to accept this request," she added, then glanced over as if to check with me. It seemed she meant to cede the final judgment. It was apparent this would be a bone-crunching schedule, but I couldn't say it was absolutely impossible.

A week, huh…? Wait. Assuming we pause operations on Saturday and Sunday, and today's date… I tried to count out the exact number of days, but I just couldn't do the calculations right. Huhhh? Has Little Hachiman always been this bad at math?

Well, the accurate numbers were in my head, but my heart would not accept them.

"Hey, just tell me this—," I said. "How many more days left do we have until the deadline…?"

"Um…" Yuigahama looked up at the ceiling with a vacant expression, sticking up one, two fingers as she began to count. Then her expression twisted up— *Erk!*

Yukinoshita looked at us with eyes filled with grief. "…I think you will feel more hopeful if you don't count."

"If you're saying that, then hope's already long gone…," I moaned.

When I was glance-glance-glancing over at Isshiki, suggesting this would be a no-go, even her expression was grim.

"…So…we can't after all?" she muttered brokenly, her voice fragile as if restraining sobs. Her eyes welled up, her breath hot. Her fists clenched around her skirt trembled slightly. Her thin shoulders twitched, and then slowly, timidly, her eyes gazed into mine. Each and every one of those gestures was filled with fervent emotion, making me want to do something for her.

But none of that! I'm already used to that sort of tearful persuasion from my sister Komachi! If you grew up with her, you'd gain immunity to it whether you liked it or not! And I'm used to accepting her pleas without hesitation.

"So we just have to make it work over the next few days, huh…?" I automatically replied in the same way as I normally did with Komachi. This big brother nature of mine was the worst!

"Thanks *sooo* much!" Isshiki beamed at me.

Meanwhile, though, the girl beside her gave me an ice-cold look, then blew out a deep sigh. "…You're always so soft."

"C-come on, now… That's one of Hikki's strong suits…and his short-comings," Yuigahama said. Just when I was thinking she'd intervened for my sake, the uncomfortable smile on her face turned into a frigid look.

Uh, I'm really sorry…for causing you trouble… I almost apologized to both of them reflexively. But Isshiki had brought this on us in the first place. *It's not my fault. It's hers!* I looked over to Isshiki to see her heaving a sigh of relief. Not that there was much on her chest to heave.

"Ohhh, you guys are *such* a big help! I've been counting on it, you know."

The admirable attitude evaporated, and she did a total 180, beaming like she was smugly pleased with herself. *Well, I kind of saw this coming anyway. Whatever.*

But if she's going to put on an act, I wish she'd keep up her coy antics right to the end! Good grief, there are no hopes or dreams.

X   X   X

It was going to be difficult to make the deadline, but we somehow had managed to set out a schedule. Our progress would affect costs, but the budget was fine at the current stage.

However, we had not decided the most important part: what we were doing.

"Well then, let's get this planning meeting *staaarted*!" Isshiki cried, drawing out her words, and Yuigahama was the only one to offer light applause. Though Isshiki took the lead at the start, a heartbeat later, she was looking over at Yukinoshita as if to say, *What should we do?*

With Isshiki's gaze on her, Yukinoshita put her hand to her chin thoughtfully. "I would suppose we should begin by considering the concept."

"Can't we just go with what Iroha-chan proposed?" asked Yuiga-hama. "Like, featuring local spots and good restaurants."

"Oh, yes! I think that's a good idea! The best plan would be something where we can use up the funds on 'research'!"

Although it seemed that Isshiki completely agreed with Yuigaha-ma's opinion, I got the impression she had ulterior motives...

Yukinoshita gave a little shake of her head. "If we had spare time, that would be enough, but given the situation, it will be hard to fill eight pages. We have to think of other articles, too."

"Is there anything else you want to do?" Yuigahama asked Isshiki.

Isshiki folded her arms, flopping her head from side to side. After a full few minutes of moaning, she muttered, "...Not really."

Yukinoshita's shoulders slumped, while Yuigahama pulled a strained smile. What else did you expect them to do?

Beginning with a concept, as Yukinoshita suggested, was very much the standard mode of attack. A concept should have led us to conclude that we needed to publish a free magazine. These were the logical steps to make something. However, for Isshiki, the publication was the goal, and the concept was an afterthought.

Right now, we needed to figure out what the readers would gain from the final output, not about what we wanted to communicate as the creators.

"If we don't know where to start, wouldn't it be faster to calculate backward from the goal?" I suggested.

"Excuse me?" I must not have articulated this well, as Isshiki tilted her head at an angle, looking at me with narrowed eyes.

This girl is so aggravating… I'm trying to help you out here, you know…

Even if I wasn't getting across to Isshiki, it seemed Yukinoshita had picked up on my intentions. "By *goal*, you mean the readers?"

"Yeah. I mean we should target our audience and make something they want to read."

"The readers… We're just handing these out at school, right?" Yuigahama asked, and Isshiki nodded.

Well, I didn't know how it would work out down the road, but for now, it should be reasonable to have a prerelease version or launch version or whatever be disseminated within the school.

Our target audience was starting to vaguely come together, so I narrowed it down further. "And it's gonna be released in March, right? The third-years will be graduating. So our main targets will be current first- and second-years."

"Depending on how often we put out issues, the new students might also be included in our target audience," added Yukinoshita.

"Ohhh, I seem to remember the incoming class is usually eager for this type of thing!" said Yuigahama.

"That's true—new students would pick it up out of curiosity," Isshiki agreed.

All three of their opinions were converging in the same direction. Meaning our main readership had been decided.

Having narrowed down our audience, we'd just have to plan with that in mind while adjusting our goals to meet these expectations.

Yukinoshita paused her note-taking, looking over what she'd written. "If our target is going to be incoming students, the issue can revolve around introducing our school with one segment to feature local spots… It just might work."

"It's admittedly generic, but it's a safe choice for a first issue," I said. "Slap on the appropriate title to tie it all together, and it should look pretty legit. Something like *A Guidebook for Your New Life*."

"Ohhh, sounds legit…" Yuigahama was impressed.

Isshiki seemed satisfied, too, clapping her hands in agreement. "I like that! So then what do we do to introduce the school?" She looked between me and Yukinoshita with expectation.

But Yukinoshita just shot her a dull look, implying that she needed to think for herself.

Ohhh, brutal…

Isshiki faltered under Yukinoshita's cold gaze, and she gave little glances over at the other girl. "It could…promote the clubs or something, I guess? …I guess?" Isshiki seemed to shrink in size, squeezing her hands against her chest.

On the other hand, Yukinoshita listened without a word, nonverbally asking if she really thought that was adequate.

And then there was Yuigahama, watching the exchange with an anxious expression.

A momentary silence dominated the clubroom. The tension rendered Isshiki speechless and a little choked up from tears.

Stop iiit! I can't watch this! Give her the right answer—stat!

I don't know if my wishes got through, but a smile finally broke on Yukinoshita's face. "…Well, I suppose that's fine." Sweeping her hair off her shoulders, she nodded.

Beside her, Isshiki let out a sigh of relief. "Then it's settled. Okey-doke, then we're introducing clubs. Clubs, hmm? Clubs…"

Nodding like all was fine and dandy, Yuigahama started scribbling the names of a bunch of clubs.

Yukinoshita popped over to take a peek at her notes. "Even just this should be enough. I think we can fill two pages."

"I wish it could take up another page," I said.

Eight pages didn't seem like much, except it was. The reader took no notice of it, but trying to fill all of them took time. When we worked on one page in the community magazine, we'd struggled. A lot.

"Yes…," Yukinoshita agreed. "It may be a good idea to select a club for a feature article to keep with the general theme."

"The tennis club!" I called out.

"The soccer club!" Isshiki responded at just about the same instant. We glared at each other.

"It's got to be the tennis club! Everyone wants to join." Look, everyone reads *Prince of Tennis*, and I get this feeling the sport is more popular lately.

But Isshiki wasn't backing down from her side, either. "It's *clearly* got to be the soccer club. That's what everyone wants to see: Hayama," she preached with sincerity.

O-okay… Name dropping Hayama weakened my argument… It was true that his photo would earn the free magazine a good reception. I knew Minami Sagami would gleefully steal multiple copies. And then Miura would wait for when nobody was around and sneakily take just one. Oh, but if Totsuka's photo were in it, I'm sure everyone would— Wait no, I take that back. I want to keep that just for me!

As I was moaning and battling this dilemma in my heart, Yuigahama looked a bit uncomfortable with the idea. "Hmm. If just one club got preferential treatment, people might complain…"

"Ahhh, yeah, some people might not be happy about that," I agreed. *Just the sort of thoughtfulness I'd expect from you, Yuigahama.* Nice thinkingahama.

Even if we didn't intent to, we didn't know how others would take it. If we wanted to avoid unnecessary quarrels, it would be easier to take the safe route to use the same template for everyone.

It seemed Isshiki had a different opinion. She knit her eyebrows and bent her mouth in an upside-down V, making her displeasure clear. "Whaaat? Can't you just ignore the haters?"

Ohhh, she's hard-hearted… But Isshiki was right. Someone was bound to complain, no matter what we did.

With a short sigh, Yukinoshita turned back to Isshiki. "We can't do that. This is an official publication by the student council. It would be best to have a measure of consideration... Since the one who will field these complaints is you." Though her words were cold, the way she said them expressed gentle concern for Isshiki.

"...I mean, that's true."

It seemed Isshiki picked up that Yukinoshita was saying this out of consideration for her. Isshiki reluctantly nodded. Though it wasn't so easy to tell, Yukinoshita was doing her best to be supportive of her juniors.

The other good upperclassman, Yuigahama, chirped, "Oh, so, like, Hayato is the chairman of the captains' association. What if the feature was on the club captains?"

Isshiki whipped up her face, and she flashed a big smile. "That's a great idea! I'll interview him!"

"All right, then let's fill a page with that interview article," suggested Yukinoshita.

Now that we had a plan, we just had to take that down to the specifics.

On the list of clubs, Yukinoshita wrote down items like *name*, then *photo* and *comments* and other things we wanted to request of them, and put it all together.

Attentively watching her take notes, Isshiki suddenly commented, "What about the Service Club?"

Yukinoshita and Yuigahama raised their heads and exchanged a look. Whether they were checking with each other or just confused, there was a moment of silence.

I ended it. "We don't have to put in this club."

"Why not?" Isshiki asked with a tilt of her head.

"Why not? I mean..." Her gaze was so direct, I found myself not knowing how to respond. To overcompensate for going quiet, I forced myself to say something I didn't really mean.

"It's kind of embarrassing to write about ourselves…"

Yuigahama nodded. "Urk, that's true…"

"I mean, nobody knows about this club anyway, so no one's exactly looking to read about it," I continued.

Yukinoshita put her hand to her chin. "Hmm, it's not as if we're actively recruiting, either…"

"Right? And besides, if we can reduce our workload by even one thing, we can focus on editing."

Even as I said that, I knew my real reason was different.

It was simply that I didn't know what to write. How could I explain this club or define it? I still didn't know the answer.

I was ready to make some more excuses, but Isshiki's sigh cut me off. "…Well, if that's your rationale, then I guess that's that."

It seemed I'd won her over. Isshiki cracked open her notebook and flipped through it, before turning back to Yukinoshita and Yuigahama. "Is this basically okay, content-wise?"

"Yes. And then about the locations to be featured…," Yukinoshita started.

Isshiki pulled her phone out of her pocket. "Ohhh, I've already looked into that! These are my photos of the places!"

"Ohhh, I wanna see!" Yuigahama peered over. Naturally, Yukinoshita, sandwiched between them, also looked at Isshiki's phone, though she seemed cramped.

Isshiki's finger swiped across the screen. With each swipe, I heard girlish remarks like "Cute!" or "Nice" or "Could you show me that photo just one more time? Yes, the one with the cat merch."

Sitting in my chair away from them, I listened to the excited chatter as I zoned out on my own phone.

And then suddenly, their conversation stopped.

Curious, I glanced over at them, and Isshiki had this *Uh-oh* look on her face. Yuigahama and Yukinoshita were shooting daggers in my direction.

"Uh, what...?" I asked.

"Ah, um, well, like, I—I was just thinking I'd like to go, too..." Yuigahama laughed, while Yukinoshita beamed at me.

"...You look like you're enjoying yourself in that photo."

Are you guys cold in here? Brr! It's freezing! I hope they fix the heater soon...

×   ×   ×

There was the click of a cup being set down on the saucer.

"Well then, it seems we already have source material for those locations," said Yukinoshita.

"Yep!" Isshiki answered as she put away her phone. It seemed she intended to use the photos from our expedition for the free magazine. Or so Isshiki explained, and though I don't know how Yukinoshita and Yuigahama took that, I was freed from their icy stares.

"So then Iroha-chan will be in charge of this," Yuigahama said, making a circle on the notepad.

We'd decided on the content. Now for the division of labor. It wasn't just assigning pages; we also needed to pick roles.

Yukinoshita summed up what was written on the notepad. "I'll handle page composition, schedule management, and design. Yuigahama, you handle interviewing the clubs and editorial stuff."

"Roger!" Yuigahama answered with energy.

Yukinoshita nodded back at her, then glanced over at me. "And Hikigaya..."

"I'll be the cameraman."

Taking photos of the clubs meant I could legally take pictures of Totsuka. I was totally raring to go, like, *Leave the camera work to me, snap-snap-snap*, but Yukinoshita's response was a merciless one.

"Writing, interviews, photography, planning, production, proof-reading, client relations, accounting, and miscellaneous tasks."

That's a lot of responsibility...and things that seem irrelevant! I made sure she knew I was disgruntled.

Yukinoshita shot me a nasty look. "Problem?"

Not a specific one. I have a problem with everything, I was thinking, when Yuigahama tap-tapped on Yukinoshita's shoulder.

"H-hey now, Yukinon. Look, he's already handled the data collection on those locations...," she mediated.

Yukinoshita didn't seem quite happy, but she let out a little sigh and flipped her hair. "...Fine. Well then, just writing and miscellaneous tasks is enough."

"...Roger."

As I nodded, I also went *Capisce!* with a sideways ☆ peace sign to acknowledge—in my head. Well, it would be fastest for me to handle the wordsmithery. It'd take us longer to proofread if Yuigahama or Isshiki wrote it, and I feel like Yukinoshita would be too formal in her writing.

With each of our roles decided, we were ready to get started. Isshiki timidly raised her hand. "Ummm, what should I do?"

"You're editor-in-chief, of course," Yukinoshita answered instantly.

"Ohhh...that sounds real cool." Yuigahama gave a smattering of applause as to celebrate.

Well, Isshiki had been the one to come up with this, so it was reasonable for her to have the job with the most responsibility. However, it seemed the one in question didn't know about that last part, and she was tilting her head to the side. "What should the editor-in-chief do?"

Yukinoshita sighed in resignation. "Yes... First, get permission to publish information and photos of these businesses."

"Right! I'll go check!" Isshiki exclaimed. Morale was high, it seemed.

Yukinoshita added, "And secure a channel for distribution. Have you already decided where they will be handed out?"

"In front of the student council room, and, like, in front of the teachers' room and places with high foot traffic?"

"Then go get permission to use those."

"Right! I'm going to tell Miss Hiratsuka."

"And if I could ask you to make copies of this on your way back?"

Isshiki accepted the notepad from Yukinoshita and clasped it tight to her chest, then saluted us, palm out. "Right! Understood! …Wait, are you just sending me on odd jobs?" Her shoulders slumped.

Ahhh, busted.

"General supervision and permissions, negotiation with outside parties, the final check, and appropriate support are all your job," Yukinoshita explained.

Isshiki sounded like she was impressed, then stood up. "Theeen I'll go tell Miss Hiratsuka!"

"Thank you."

As Isshiki was passing by me in order to leave the clubroom, she grabbed me by the sleeve. "Let's go."

"Uh, go by yourself…"

"If you're with me, you can be like a lightning rod—whoops, I mean lead to lightning-fast ideas, right?! And you're reliable!"

You didn't have to correct yourself… But as she said, I do have a reputation for being a lightning rod. If my presence would make the conversation go smoothly, then I would just pop over there and get it done with.

"Guess I'll go, then." Slipping out of her grasp on my sleeve, I left my chair.

Then there was some scraping of chairs as Yuigahama stood. "Oh, then I'll go, too!"

"Agh… If we're to explain the materials, it would be best for me to go, wouldn't it?" Yukinoshita sighed, then quietly got up from her own chair.

"Okay! Let's all go together!" Yuigahama grabbed hold of both Yukinoshita's and Isshiki's arms, then briskly headed for the door.

Hmm, body heat seems like a good defense for the cold hallway…

Well, if all three of them were coming, I could probably just stand there and do nothing. Following the girls, I left the clubroom behind.

×　×　×

Upon entering the teachers' room, I headed straight for Miss Hiratsuka's desk.

Among the rows of desks, I discovered her sitting at one that was particularly messy. She was in front of her computer, clattering away on the keyboard as she occasionally drew soba out from the take-out bowl at her side.

Eating again, huh…? "Miss Hiratsuka."

"Hmm? Ohhh, it's you, Hikigaya. Why's everyone here?"

"We wanted to ask about something…"

"Hmm? Mmm." Miss Hiratsuka glanced over at the bowl, then paused as if considering a bit.

"We won't mind if you keep eating," Yukinoshita told her.

"Oh? Sorry." Miss Hiratsuka gave an apologetic laugh, then picked up the bowl. Spinning her chair around to turn her profile to us, she took her chopsticks in hand. After slurping up some soba, she prompted us to continue. "So then what were you asking about?"

"We were thinking about making a free magazine," said Isshiki.

Surprised, Miss Hiratsuka dubiously parroted, "A free magazine?"

Isshiki began to explain the plan to publish it. With Yukinoshita supplementing where necessary, we showed the teacher the summary, the pamphlet, and the estimate.

"We've already gotten a quote," Yukinoshita explained, "and it's possible to get this within the budget. As for the content, we've put a general plan together. It's still rough, though."

"Hmm." While occasionally slurping on her soba, Miss Hiratsuka examined the materials with interest. After flipping through the papers, she seemed to get the gist and raised her head again. "Well, you're totally free to do it... But couldn't you do it on straw paper, using a mimeograph?"

Yuigahama tilted her head. "Straw paper?"

"What? Mimeograph?" Isshiki gave Miss Hiratsuka an unconvinced look—actually, it was just downright rude.

This girl has a serious attitude problem...

In normal circumstances, this was Miss Hiratsuka's cue to offer educational guidance, but it seemed she didn't have the energy. "Oh, you've never heard of those...," she muttered weakly, breaking into this worn, bitter, somehow self-deprecating smile.

"I've heard of them, but I've never seen them in real life...," Yukinoshita admitted apologetically, as if finishing her off.

"Of course...," Miss Hiratsuka answered, voice trembling slightly.

It was inevitable, seeing how advancements in machinery and paper improved by the day. And hey, a mimeograph? Even at her age, I doubted she's seen the real thing... Uh, though I obviously didn't know her age.

And then said thirtyish woman of unknown age slumped over, cradling her bowl. "Well, just give it a shot," she muttered and offered nothing more as she sadly began to slurp her now soggy soba...

×   ×   ×

Now that we had received permission from Miss Hiratsuka, finally, we began the actual work.

I borrowed another laptop so that we could all deal with the tasks allotted to us, and I began typing up what we needed.

That was when Yukinoshita ambled over to me. "Hikigaya, do you have a moment?"

"Uh-huh," I replied, and she sat down diagonally across from me, spreading out the transmittal form. The transmittal form is, simply put, a summary listing the composition of each page and the assigned editor.

Yukinoshita tapped one corner of the draft. "The problem is what to do with the cover page."

"Wouldn't it be easiest just to avoid the problem with a simple design or photo?"

"Or a picture with a caption and something like a logo or a border around it?"

"Yeah, I figure it just has to look like we got inspo from *Time* or *Forbes*."

"Yes, I think making an obvious homage might make it more aesthetic."

"And that'll shave off some time."

As we were talking, I felt eyes on us from a distance. Isshiki was looking at us with an expression of pure horror. "I have no idea what you two are talking about…"

"Yeah? Me neither!" Yuigahama admitted, leaning over her desk.

She seemed almost glad to have company…? The two buddies were right in the middle of making a form to request comments from the clubs. We had our own discussion to move along.

Yukinoshita was making notes in the layout draft when her hand paused, and she brought her pen to smoosh into her cheek. "So that's our design direction. The question is the subject matter."

"We can just go with a photo of Isshiki. She's the president, after all." I jabbed my thumb in the direction of the girl in question.

Isshiki waved her hands wildly. "Huh? You mean, like, gravure? Swimsuits are off the table for me."

"Who cares... And hey, we never asked you to do that." *Just what else is off the table for her...?*

I could see she was playing up her coy act to seem purer. When you get to my level, you stop believing in terms like *the girl next door*, or *amateur*, or *magic mirror*.

"...Oh, really?" Isshiki must have been offended, as her voice was weirdly cold, and there was a sharpness to the flash in her narrowed eyes. She pulled her lips in a tight downward V, putting her hand to her chest as she considered awhile. Eventually, she got this nasty smirk like she'd had an idea, then did an about-face. "*Okaaay* then, who *are* you asking to do it? *Ohhh*, Yui?"

"H-hey! I—I can't do that! No way! Absolutely no way!" With Isshiki yanking her, Yuigahama pitched forward, and her skin peeked out from her loose collar, emphasizing her chest. I felt myself magnetically drawn to it, but with force of will, I tore my eyes away.

I won't give in! I can't give in to temptation!

I somehow managed to lift my gaze, but then our eyes met. Yuigahama's cheeks were bright red, and she hugged her shoulders as if hiding her body. "Ah, I mean...th-that stuff is too embarrassing... There's no way... People seeing me like that would be too much..." She paused between words, turning her face away. She was red to the neck. Once she was done talking, she flicked me this little questioning glance, and her eyes seemed hot, too.

Frankly, I feel like a certain sector would very much enjoy seeing her on the cover, but I don't think I'd find that situation pleasant. I mean, look, she doesn't want to do it, all right? "Uh, I wouldn't... Like, I'd never do...something like that."

"R-really? ...Oh, good." Yuigahama seemed relieved, her shoulders relaxing. I let go of some tension as well, letting out a deep sigh.

Once Yuigahama had calmed down, I hit on the reason the conversation had gone in this direction. "And wait, *gravure* doesn't mean swimsuit photography. I think, like, printing a page of photos? Or something like that is called gravure."

Right? Miss Yukipedia? I turned to Yukinoshita. She'd been fiddling with her ribbon tie this whole time, but when my eyes met with hers, she jerked her gaze away. Then she retied her ribbon. "..."

I heard a faint sigh. *I wish she would stop going silent at moments like these...*

"Anyway, a normal uniform photo is fine. Okay, next. Yukinoshita, what do we do about the back cover?" I changed the topic, and Yukinoshita narrowed her eyes at me for just a second. It seemed that despite her lack of reply, she did basically intend to listen.

I just went on ahead. "Will we put ads in? Like for mysterious prayer beads, or speed-reading techniques, or exercise machines, or health goods," I said, irresponsibly imagining pictures of Zaimokuza in a bathtub full of cash.

Finally, Yukinoshita spoke up. "It's not realistic to start searching for places that would advertise with us this late. If we're going to continue publishing this in the future, then it would be fine to look into it, but it's not feasible this time, at least. Since we don't have material, we should fill the space with written content," she said dispassionately, eyes still on the layout.

I considered a bit. "Something like a column, or an editor's note? ...Well, I'll handle that stuff."

"Yes, please do," Yukinoshita replied briefly, and then as usual, she began carrying out her task without looking at me. The scratching of her ballpoint pen was particularly loud.

Dear me, is she still bothered by that earlier conversation…? It's not like there's anything to worry about…

It's okay! There's still hope! Genetically speaking, of course!

X   X   X

I was tasked with writing and taking photos, which was the job I'd asked for. That meant I needed to interview the clubs. There wasn't much time, so we were splitting into two groups for the job: me and Isshiki, then Yuigahama and Yukinoshita. If you took an average of our communication and academic skills, then, well, it was a fair way to divide us up. We went for the boys' clubs, while Yukinoshita and Yuigahama would be mainly interviewing the girls' clubs.

Our first subject for interview was, of course…the tennis club!

Yuigahama had handled making the appointment beforehand, so Isshiki and I just went down to the tennis court, where the cold winds whistled by.

"Your receive is slow! You can try a little harder!" The cute voice that rang across the court was that of the tennis club captain, Totsuka. Racket over one shoulder and the other hand on his waist, he was pushing the younger members. It seemed Mr. Captain was now good and used to the job.

When we came up to the side of the court, Totsuka noticed us and waved a hand as he came trotting over. "Hachiman! And Isshiki! Hello."

"Sorry for bothering you." Matching Isshiki as she gave an extra-polite bow, I also gave a wave in greeting.

"Oh, no, it's totally fine! Um, you were going to take pictures? Go ahead anytime." Totsuka gave a little shake of his head, then spread his arms and spun around, gesturing to the tennis court. Then he turned his head to me and smiled.

Yep, I'd say I'm all ready!

"Then let's get right to it…," I said.

Totsuka with his arms spread was cute, so that was the first shot. I raised the camera and snapped the shutter. Then Totsuka seemed confused, so one more. Then he tilted his head cutely, so I took another. And then as I was raising the camera again to get a photo of Totsuka's curious expression, he started to talk to me. "Umm…weren't you taking pictures of practice?"

"That too. But first, this," I declared—quite boldly, openly, and emphatically, for me.

Totsuka seemed overwhelmed by the force of my remark, as he faltered slightly. "O-oh…I'm a little embarrassed… Hmm…"

Shy about having his picture taken, he put his hands to his face to hide his blushing, looking indecisive, but then he glanced over to the tennis court. "But if new students see this, they might join the club…"

"Yeah, the new students might read this to get information," I said. Yuigahama had told him about the aim of this free magazine when she had made the appointment. This would also be a good opportunity for the clubs to get exposure.

Totsuka lifted his head resolutely. "I-I'll do my best…" Then he clenched a little fist in front of his chest to get himself fired up.

"O-okay then…let's do our best." It was good that I'd managed to win over Totsuka, but despite my own words, I was feeling like I'd used smooth talk to lure him into a photo shoot. *Why do I feel so guilty…? No, wait. This feeling isn't guilt… It's the feeling of corruption! This is actually getting me more motivated, in a way!*

"Okay, let me keep snapping these photos."

"Yeah!" he answered with spirit, and I raised the camera.

"This time, try holding up the racket."

"O-okay."

I got a shot of Totsuka swinging the racket from a low angle, then a dynamic shot of him taking a step forward, and then when he lost his balance, I captured him in my finder again. A perfect shot!

I got all the photos of Totsuka in motion I wanted, and the photo session moved on to the next stage.

"Okay, try hugging the racket next."

"Uh-huh… Huh?" Totsuka cocked his head in puzzlement but nevertheless squeezed the racket tight to his chest. I got a photo burst, hot shots, and then even a panorama shot. As an option, we added a towel. *Nice, nice, let's get a little bolder*, I thought while enthusiastically snapping photos.

Off to the side, Isshiki was quite severely disturbed. "Isn't that enough…?"

"Is it? Well, I guess."

"It is." She nodded emphatically.

Indeed, she had a point. "You're right—that's enough for the racket. Okay, then let's go without the racket."

"What?" Isshiki froze on the spot.

But I ignored her, peering through the finder as I planned out the next stage of the shoot. "You all right, Totsuka?"

"…Yeah." His response was a little dispirited. Maybe he was getting worn-out.

It was kind of like when my cat got tired of all the attention. In other words, Totsuka is just that cute!

Under my instructions, Totsuka put the racket at his feet and sat down, hugging his knees. I took shots from different angles, from the front to the left diagonal. I had him make various poses, alternating looking at the camera and away. For shots where he was looking at the camera, I got him both smiling and showing ennui.

"H-Hachiman…are we done?" Totsuka asked, his smile strained and voice stuttering.

"O-oh, yeah…" It did seem he was a bit fatigued. *What should I do…?* I thought, and it hit me. "Let's break for a bit."

"There's more…?" His shoulders slumped.

Mm-hmm, it seems my decision to take a break was not mistaken after all. As I was making camera adjustments to prepare for the second half, checking the photos I'd taken so far, I had a terrible realization.

"Isshiki," I called out to her.

She must already have gotten sick of dealing with me, as she was standing quite a ways apart from us, watching from a distance. She dragged herself over to me like this was a huge pain. "What is it?"

"You don't have any extra memory cards? We're out of space."

"How many photos have you taken…?"

"I've actually deleted the extras, you know…"

Isshiki sighed. Then she grabbed a fistful of my blazer sleeve and began dragging me away.

"That's enough! Totsuka, thank you for your time," she called out.

Totsuka stopped cradling his knees, snapping his head up to smile at us. "Oh, okay. I should thank you guys, really."

I would very much have liked to capture that smile in a photo, but Isshiki was yanking me away, so I would not get my hot shot or my photo burst. And so, to capture it in the photo album of my mind, I captured one last shot in my heart.

X   X   X

With Isshiki pulling me along by the sleeve, we headed for the soccer club.

Their practice was out on the sports field right beside the tennis court, so it wasn't much of a trip. Good thing, because I wasn't much of a fan of their club.

I figured I'd just take two or three easy photos and go, but Isshiki was not letting that happen.

"Oh, right around there, please center Hayama in your shot. Oh, right now, go!" Tap-tapping on my shoulder, she gave me minute instructions on exactly when to take pictures. And then when I was done, she checked over the photos. "Show me, please… Oh, Tobe wound up in this one. Delete!" she announced, erasing the photo and shoving the camera back at me.

Well, whatever, if it's just Tobe… Nobody will care whether he makes it in.

This sort of thing went on for quite some time, which meant we didn't make much progress.

"Hey, haven't we done enough?" I said. "There's no more space…"

"And whose fault is that?" Isshiki puffed up her cheeks as she glared at me out of the corner of her eye. I didn't really have a good comeback. In the end, I was forced to take photos the whole time, until the scrimmage was over.

When they were finally done with their practice game, Hayama walked over to us.

"Hayamaaaa!" Isshiki called, waving, and he casually waved back in response.

"I did hear the broad strokes from Yui. She says you're making a free magazine? I see you're doing whatever people ask of you again." Though he wore a charming smile, there was a flicker of exasperation in his voice.

"Like I've said," I told him, "that's just what the job is. And I don't wanna hear that from someone who left his club early to get interviewed. Sorry for bothering you."

"That's a weird way to thank me." Hayama shrugged and smiled, then turned his face toward the courtyard. "You must be cold. Why don't we do the interview over there?"

"Ah, good idea."

The courtyard piloti area was enclosed by the school building, so the wind couldn't get in. With a beaming smile, Isshiki took the lead, heading for a spot that looked good. Right beside the vending machine was a bench, though a simple one. Isshiki sat down, patting the spot beside herself to beckon Hayama. *So calculated…*

I let Hayama go on ahead while I bought a can of black coffee and some black tea at the vending machine. Juggling the scorching cans, I stood opposite from Hayama.

"You just have to say whatever sounds good. You're good at that, aren't you?" I asked, tossing the coffee at Hayama.

Catching it, he looked at the can with surprise, but then he let out a little whiff of a sigh and chuckled wryly. "Are you being sarcastic?"

"That was totally a compliment. Whatever. Thanks for taking us up on this."

"…Well, I'll do my best to meet your expectations," Hayama said, breaking into a broad smile. Then he lightly raised one hand to me and turned back to Isshiki.

"Well then, let's get this interview started!" Isshiki activated the audio recorder on her phone, and I set down the tea beside her, then backed up about two steps and raised the camera to get a shot.

The Hayama beyond my finder was, as I'd known he would be, the same Hayato Hayama everyone knew—but he seemed a little different from the boy who had just been joking with a wry smile.

× × ×

We finished Hayama's interview and photography session, following which we went around to a number of clubs, and then the interviewing and photography for the clubs we were supposed to be handling was done. I'd managed to get a photo of Hayama doing that gesture like he was spinning a pottery wheel, so when it came to the ratio of usable footage, it should be good.

Yuigahama and Yukinoshita had been mostly handling the girls' clubs and would be done soon, by this time. Then the only picture left to take would be of Iroha Isshiki, who would decorate the cover of the free magazine.

At the request of the model for this shoot, we would do it in the library.

We circled from the courtyard around to the front entrance, swapped into our indoor shoes, and passed in front of the teachers' room to head to the library.

Once it got a little late after school, there were hardly any students using the library, and it was peaceful.

"So why here…?" I asked Isshiki's back.

She was doing a full lap of the space, walking around searching for the best photo spot. When I asked that question, she spun around to face me.

"Makes me seem more intellectual, right?"

"And what you just said makes you seem *less* intellectual…"

"It's fine. I only need the image." She stuck her nose in the air, then started walking again, pausing many times.

She seemed to finally reach a decision and sat down at an available table with a bookshelf behind her. Then she took out a compact mirror and began cheerfully checking her looks.

The tall bookshelf towered over her protectively, the dark colors of the book spines casting her in sharp relief. Perhaps so people could read comfortably, the library was bright, even close to nighttime, giving Isshiki's pale skin a warm glow.

Being an amateur, I couldn't really delve into further detail, but still, Isshiki had created the picture-perfect image. As expected of Iroha Isshiki—I guess this means she knows how to make herself look attractive.

"Okay. Let me take a few," I said to her, and instead of a reply, she posed herself with her chin in her hand, elbow on the desk.

Her puppy-dog eyes examined me invitingly, emphasizing her dewy pupils and long eyelashes, and the little proud smile on her lips had a lingering innocence, despite the alluring pink of her soft lips.

Though I was properly pointing the lens at her, I'd forgotten to click the shutter. I heard someone clear their throat and shook myself out of it.

After I snapped a few photos, I lowered the camera. And then, while checking over the data I'd just taken, to cover how I'd been zoning out, I said, "You're used to being photographed, huh...?"

Isshiki was right in the middle of looking in the mirror, considering various options as she attempted a new pose. She tilted her head at her reflection. "You think? Isn't it normal to take pictures all the time?"

"Not all the time." I think trips, events, and special times are the kinds of things to commemorate, and we do that with pictures. At the very least, that's what I've been taught.

But Isshiki was saying something completely different. She snapped her compact mirror shut and glanced over at me, and though my camera was not pointed at her, she had on a soft smile. "But memories are important, right?"

That was normal to Iroha Isshiki.

She said she made no distinction between the mundane and the extraordinary, and that even the same old sights of nothing new or special were precious memories to be embraced.

"...Yeah."

With only that brief reply, I once again raised the camera, thinking...

All right, is this photo a memory of the mundane, or a record of the extraordinary?

X   X   X

A few days had passed since we'd assembled most of the material and commenced production. We were making progress on the club introductions and the hot spot guides, and the interview article was mostly done. The design work was also going smoothly, filling up pages from the cover onward.

The articles would be just about done, after some adjustments like adding in minor captions and massaging the headlines. And the comments from the captains were mostly there with some minor text corrections.

It was going well. Or it should have been.

I'd done a neat job with the club introduction text, the articles on the recommended spots, the audio tape transcription of the interviews, and the translation of those in Isshiki-speak. We had gotten the clubs to check over the photos we'd taken. And even with the cover, when Isshiki had said she wanted it photoshopped, I had safely settled the matter with some soothing and coaxing.

But. *But*, for some reason, my writing was still not done.

"How did this happen…?"

Was it because I had been taking this seriously? It's true I'd been hard at work. I had not only done the writing of the regular article page, I had also helped out Yukinoshita, and I had gone to prompt the UG Club for comments in Yuigahama's stead.

I'd spent these past few days diligently and busily, for me. Perhaps that was why…so occupied in the flurry, I had carelessly forgotten other work…

We had two days until the deadline! I still had the whole column to do.

As I was holding my head in my hands in despair, Isshiki, standing beside me, poured some tea out of a plastic bottle and offered it to me. "Here you go. Good luck," she said, putting the plastic bottle away in the mini fridge under the desk. She sat herself down diagonally across from me.

The tea was different from usual, the desk was different from usual, the chair was different from usual. And the room was a different one from usual, too.

I was presently being confined to the student council room, where, under surveillance, I was to write the column. The heater in the club-room still wasn't fixed yet, so Isshiki had very kindly offered the student council room to be my personal prison.

I glanced out the window and saw it was already evening. Even if I wanted to know the exact time, my cell phone had been confiscated, so there was no way for me to know. When I swept my gaze across the student council room, the table clock pointed to a cruel number.

I had not taken one step out of here since I'd been brought to this room immediately after school. The reason was: The deadline was the next day.

Waughhh, this is bad... I haven't written anything... I can't imagine making this in time...

I just typed away on the keyboard to get the words down, but I wasn't satisfied with them and erased them halfway. I kept doing it over and over. *Oh man, ohhhh man. I'm not gonna make it at this raaaate!*

Seeing me flail in panic at my desk, Isshiki leaned away in disgust. Her expression seemed to want to say, *Eugh...* She was giving little shakes of her head, but then she seemed to notice something with a jolt, and she fished around in her blazer pocket.

"You've got a call," she said, taking my cell phone out of her pocket to hold it out to me.

But when a phone call comes to you when you're right before a deadline, there's no way it can be anything good. I mean, if you can force something to exist, anime would never need recap episodes, and the postponement of on-sale dates due to authors' personal circumstances wouldn't be a thing.

So when you get a call at a time like this, it's best to check who it is, then ignore it.

"…From who? Editorial?" I asked.

Isshiki sighed in exasperation. "If *Editorial* is the first thing out of your mouth, you must be stressed, huh…? Um… Ah, it says *Mom*. Is that your mom?"

"…From Editorial's mom? …Their whole family is gonna come monitor me?"

"No? Why would that happen? It's from *your* mom, probably."

"Oh. I'll call her back later, so you can just leave it."

"Uh-huh, is that right?" With that short reply, Isshiki tucked my phone back into her pocket. And then she flipped through a bunch of papers probably related to the closing of the accounts, checking through them and occasionally stamping.

With her doing work beside me, I started to feel like I had to work, too… Left with no choice, I began clacking away on the keyboard.

More time passed.

It was already dark outside the window, and eventually, it would be time to go home. Isshiki must have finished her task at some point, as I couldn't hear stamping anymore. When I glanced over at her, she was on her phone.

Maybe I'm good for the day, too… There's still tomorrow, after all. If I can work harder tomorrow than I did today, I could finish it…

As soon as that hit me, my focus immediately evaporated.

"It's no use. I can't write anymore today. You can't write anything good if you rush it. I have no choice but to go take a break, go home, and sleep," I declared loudly.

Lifting her face from her phone, Isshiki looked at me. She let out a sigh of exasperation, but the look on her face was kind. "Agh, *welll*, I guess it's fine."

"Right? It's fine for it to be just a bit late." I think they call it a writer's high or something. The excess pre-deadline stress, the exhaustion of continuous work, and this mysterious feeling of elation caused by escaping from reality left me laughing, "*Na-ha-ha!*"

Isshiki's face stiffened. "…Huh? You're not gonna make it?"

"W-well, who knows…"

The column was in fact just a few thousand characters, and if I worked hard that day and the next, it wasn't as if managing it was impossible. Well, given how I'd failed to write even a few hundred characters over the past few hours, it seemed unlikely.

I hesitated to speak honestly about this. As for why—because even before I'd explained anything, Isshiki was holding her head in her hands.

"That's not good… Not good at all… Ummm, that's *really* bad, isn't it?" Facedown on the desk, Isshiki moaned, then slowly looked over to me, her eyes a little dewy. She was muttering quietly to herself. "The funds…the early discount…additional fees…over budget…the year's balance…"

From her reaction, I understood. When doing up the budget, Isshiki had assumed we would make it in time for that discount plan she'd mentioned, and she'd already written it down on the annual accounting report form.

Of course, I'd assume it was possible to make adjustments to that report.

This situation had been brought about because a certain *Something-man Something-gaya* had arrogantly taken on this project and started talking big about how he would manage somehow in a few days, then put off the column he'd brought up himself by saying "Yeah, I can dash it off real quick. Easy." Getting cocky never ends well…

"…Th-this is bad, huh…? Uh-huh. I-I'll put in a bit more effort, okay?" I said.

"Y-you will? Please do…" Isshiki's eyes glimmered as she looked up at me. There was none of her usual cunning there, and I could see through to her honest self, more childish than normal.

If she's gonna show me that, then I have no choice but to do it, even if I have to force myself…

There lies the deadline I absolutely cannot fail to make.

× × ×

To tell the truth, I just can't. Sorry for saying this out of the blue. But it's the truth.

In a few hours, a very ordinary bell will ring.

That will be the signal for the deadline.

An editor with a small chest will come, so watch out.

Following which, after a brief few moments, the end will come.

I was zoning out.

I'd psyched myself up by saying I absolutely could not, would not fail to make this deadline—but the next day after school, I was yet again borrowing the use of student council space, locked alone in the room by myself until I finished the job. The after-school writing session from the day prior felt like a distant dream.

Despite having gotten a second wind the day before and tried for a while, just like Chiyonofuji in the sumo ring when he was at the limits of his strength, I had burned out and gone home. After getting home, I'd made a tiny bit more progress, and then during class, I'd written some more on my phone, but I still couldn't see the end.

And now I was looking out the window of the empty student council room, gazing up at the setting sun. Of course, I was making no progress on the draft.

Oh crap... The clack-clack was not coming from the keyboard, but from my bones as they trembled in fear.

That was when a knock came on the door of the student council room.

"How are things going, Hikki?" Yuigahama asking, clipping through the door. It seemed she'd come to check on my progress.

"...M-my conservative guess? About seventy percent."

"Oh, that's great!"

"...Left to do," I added quietly, and Yuigahama let out a tiny cry.

Same, Yuigahama. I'm screwed...

As I was hanging my head, Yuigahama approached my desk and planted a hand on my shoulder. "Let's do our best! It's okay—you'll make it in time! I'll work here with you, too!"

That just means she's going to be monitoring me...

Normally, I would refuse to work under surveillance, but the situation was what it was. I had to keep the pressure up, or I was bound to drop the ball. I mean, if this were a part-time job, I'd be flaking out, but being monitored by Isshiki the day before and then Yuigahama that day, too, I'd have to do it. There's a thing called temper for steel and men...

Finding my motivation once more, I faced the draft. I brought the cursor to my current spot so I could write from where I'd left off. And then, when I managed to wring out a few lines more, despair came to assault me yet again. Every time I looked at the blank space of the draft, I was made aware of how few characters I'd written, compared with the time that had progressed.

In one day, I had only made 20 percent progress. Filling up the remaining 80 percent in a few more hours was physically impossible; if I could make it now, then the laws of the universe meant nothing!

Wagh... As I was overcome by reality, I heard a clattering sound beside me that was different from my own typing. When I happened to look over, I saw Yuigahama sitting there, tapping into a calculator with a ballpoint pen in one hand.

"...What're you doing?" I asked her.

Sticking her red pen behind her ear, she turned to me. "Hmm? Um, adding up all the expenses. Since when I looked at it, it seemed a little rough."

"Isshiki's pretty sloppy with the bookkeeping..."

"Ahhh, yeah... Well, me and Yukinon will make sure to handle that stuff!" she said with a forced smile. It was somehow big sisterly—it seemed she was trying to do her part to take care of Isshiki, her junior.

The problem was that said cute junior often spelled trouble. I mean, like, her whole thing with coming to the clubroom was already pretty bad...

However, this is just how work is.

There's one big liar, and work comes from the process of making their big lie a reality. Out in the adult world, you call those big liars producers. In that sense, maybe you could say Isshiki was producer material. So then in terms of this whole affair, Yukinoshita was the director, and Yuigahama was the assistant director, I guess. And with this job, as always, I'd be the miserable, low-ranking, subcontracted corporate cog.

To perform my labor, as befit a menial worker, I once again faced my computer. But I just kept writing a few lines and then erasing them over and over, and I couldn't manage to make solid progress.

Eventually, I was spending more and more time gazing out the window at the sunset, or at the clock, rather than looking at the computer screen.

The passage of time alone is enough to press the spirit to the limit. And with the exhaustion of sitting at the computer for a long time, before I knew it, I was letting out a deep sigh.

"Are you okay, Hikki?" Yuigahama must have heard my big sigh, as she rose from her seat and came up a few steps to stand beside me, examining my face with concern.

Her face was so close that if I reached out, I could just about touch it. She was near enough that I could practically hear her breathe. The proximity and eye contact made me embarrassed, and thoughtlessly, I pretended to gulp and turned my head away.

"It doesn't look okay, schedule-wise...," I muttered to cover my embarrassment, when suddenly, a weight came down on my shoulder.

"If you don't make it, then we cross that bridge when we get there."

When I turned just my head around to look back at her, I found Yuigahama's small hand gently sitting on my shoulder. Her thin fingers clenched into a fist, grabbing the fabric of my blazer. "I'll apologize with you, and I think Iroha-chan will understand, too. It was kinda too much to begin with."

"Well, it's true, but...," I said, twisting around in an attempt to escape her hand, but it wouldn't move away. Eventually, she began to *tap, tap* away on my shoulder in small motions.

"It's not like it's your fault. If we abandon this now, nobody's gonna blame us. It's not like it's something we absolutely have to do, anyway."

Her remark was a little surprising. Yuigahama had never expressed negativity toward any of the requests the Service Club had accepted before.

Confused, I turned my whole body without thinking and saw a weak little smile on her face. "...I don't think I want you to have a hard time, Hikki."

"That's such an unfair thing to say."

For a comment that just popped out of my mouth, my tone was gentle enough that even I could tell. You could even call it weak and listless. If she was going to say that in such a calm voice while tapping on my shoulder, of course my shoulders would relax.

But it also built a tension in me.

I'm not yet so detached that I could back down now after a wonderful girl said that to me. The very offer of such kind and sweet words was why I could not rely on them or let myself off the hook. So no matter how stupid this whole project was, even if this had been an unreasonable ask, I couldn't leave it now.

"I guess it is unfair…" Yuigahama's hand stopped. It just gently lay on my shoulder, then eventually slowly lowered.

"Ah, I mean, that was just, like, a figure of speech." It's a bit rude to accuse ill of someone who was showing concern for you. I turned around in my chair, properly facing Yuigahama with my whole body. And then, despite my fluster, I struggled to find the appropriate way to express this.

But Yuigahama didn't wait, giving a big nod. "…Yeah, maybe I am being unfair!" she said in a bright voice with a smile, as if I'd somehow won her over.

I really couldn't figure out what that reaction meant. To communicate my intentions as precisely as possible, I said, "I didn't mean it like that. It's, like, actually in a good way, I mean…"

She gave a little shake of her head to cut me off. "I think I really am unfair… It's always like, I can't really stop you, and I can't really help you. And, well…everything else." Maybe she was thinking aloud, because she faltered frequently. But I think that just meant the words came from somewhere deep within. It's like when people speak vaguely with a shy smile or look away—there were feelings she was trying to cover up.

Nevertheless, she was looking straight at me this time.

"So… So that's why… Next time this sort of thing happens, I'll be better."

In her earnest expression and the words she delivered slowly, there was an empty vagueness that grounded me in reality. Eventually, anyone will do it right. You have to. Though you don't know how or what, or if you can do it. I'm sure anyone will be thinking something along those lines.

Of course, I'm no exception there. That was why first, for the time being, I had to do the thing in front of me. I turned my chair around and faced the computer once more.

"It's fine. I'm always just doing my own thing. You're not at fault for not stopping me. I mean, like, it's my fault for being the one who makes promises without thinking them through. So, well…I'll try to figure it out somehow."

"…Okay… Then let's do our best!" she said with cheer and gave my back an energetic push.

×   ×   ×

Ahhh, nooo! I wanna go home! I don't care! I don't care about the draft submission or the revisions or completion! I've had enough of being hounded by deadlines and being locked up to work! I'm quitting work and this draft!

Wahhh! I landed facedown on the desk. I was currently alone in the student council room, so I could scream to my heart's content.

I'd handed Yuigahama a printout of my work in progress and had her give it to Yukinoshita for me. After that, my focus had completely broken.

Well, I had somehow, some way, brought it to the 80 percent point. With that added motivation I'd gotten from Yuigahama, I think I'd tried pretty hard, for me.

However, the remaining 20 percent just wouldn't come out. I leaned into the back of my chair and looked up at the ceiling. *Ahhh, I wish the Illuminati would come down on me... I would like to be permanently banished from ever working again...!*

I believe focus is not continuous, but something that comes in short bursts. That's why pulling a couple of all-nighters is not going to push your progress ahead dramatically, and systematic progress on a regular basis is important. But there's no point in coming to that realization right before the deadline, huh? It's just like before exams, seriously.

Still staring up at the ceiling, I was zoning out like my batteries were drained when there came a knocking on the door of the student council room. Lacking the energy to answer, I just looked in that direction, but despite my lack of reply, the visitor entered.

"Are you done?" Addressing me was Yukinoshita, her bag flung over her shoulder.

"...If I were, I'd have told you."

"True," she said as if that made sense to her, and then she ambled up to me and pulled out some papers from her bag, marked up in red ink. "The printouts I just received. Right here, this is a sentence fragment that's missing the back half."

"O-okay."

I accepted the pages from her, and as I skimmed over them, a number of errors caught my eye, including the missing sentence. As I applied her corrections to my draft, I continued to feel a presence beside me. "... Did you have some business?"

"Oh, no...it's not enough to call business," Yukinoshita said, sounding a little rattled, folding her hands behind her before stepping away to pull out a chair beside me. She rummaged through her bag a moment, soon found a file folder, and pulled it out to begin some task.

It seemed she was going to work here while monitoring me. Her presence meant there was really no time before the deadline.

She didn't have to put pressure on me. I understood just fine how bad this was.

Once I was done applying the corrections from the printouts she'd given me, I scrolled down the screen to finish off the remaining 20 percent.

It was only a few hundred characters left.

If I just wrote that much, then I'd fill the space, at least.

Although that would make up the difference, if the column was shoddy, the one to get the heat for it would be the editor-in-chief, Isshiki. I couldn't accept this task so casually, then act like I didn't give a damn if she got bashed.

Ultimately, I was forced to make a completed product of a certain level of quality. Or rather, if I wrote junk, then I'd get hit with corrections from our editor, Yukinoshita, and then also from the editor-in-chief, Isshiki. Rather than getting hounded by their revisions, it would be faster to put serious effort into writing from the start.

Mustering up my final dregs of energy, I kept on typing at the keyboard. One minute, then two minutes passed on the time display under the screen as I filled line after line of white.

Eventually, my hands came to a stop, and they moved no more after that. The words slipped out of me, my voice utterly drained without my noticing. "...I'm done."

"Oh, really?" Hearing me, Yukinoshita sounded glad as she started to stand.

I raised a hand to stop her, pitching straight forward to slump my face on the desk. "No. I'm done for. I can't do it. It's no use. I can't think of anything. Not a single character will come out..."

"That's what you meant..." With an exasperated sigh, Yukinoshita sat back down in her chair. "That's a problem. We have no more time, you know?"

"Yeah, I do get that, but still..."

I understood it horribly well. But my head would just not work, no matter what. My brain had low motivation to work in the first place, so this seemed out of my control. Just as a wrung rag won't let out a single drop of water, not one more word would come out of me.

I leaned all the way back in my chair and looked up at the ceiling. I was all out of options…

My hands, curled up in front of the keyboard, would not move, but neither would they leave the keyboard. My body faced up to the ceiling, just like the corpse of a bug. *I'm an insect…an incompetent louse that can't even make it on time for a deadline. Starting tomorrow, I will go by Insect Hachiman. And then I will chuck my human card into the ocean…*

As I was staring up at the ceiling, my mind lost and abandoned, Yukinoshita slid into my field of view. Looking down at me, she seemed somehow unsettled. "…Here," she said, and she dropped something wrapped in a handkerchief on my chest.

Raising my head and picking up the bundle, I found it was slightly warm. When I opened up the handkerchief with cute cat footprints, a MAX Coffee emerged from within. It seemed she had made a basic effort to keep it warm.

Seeing this, I let a smile slip.

"Go clear your head. This isn't something that will somehow work out if you just keep staring at the screen. It's best to take a bit of a break," she advised, turning her face away, before returning to sit in her chair and resuming her task.

"Thanks…" I decided to accept the gift with gratitude. After opening the tab, I zoned out while sipping the coffee and gazed at her profile.

Yukinoshita's hands never stopped all the while. She never said a word; the only sound was the scratch of her red pen running over paper. I felt like I was hearing that sound an unusual number of times.

"…Is it that bad?" I asked.

"Huh?" She turned to face me. Then her gaze dropped to the paper in her hands. It seemed she understood what I was trying to say. She waved her red pen, then touched it to her lips as she said, "...Yes, but it's just things like typos and kanji errors. There's nothing horrendous, so don't worry. In fact, I'd say the other two had more errors." Yukinoshita giggled, as if it were a joke. She looked rather more innocent than usual, and it felt appropriate to her age.

"I mean, you've kind of been penning in a lot of red, so it made me a little anxious."

"Oh, yes, I just forgot to mention we're adding phonetics to the difficult kanji, so I'm putting it in directly myself. Just while I'm doing the revisions."

"Sorry for giving you more work."

I hadn't meant anything in saying that, but Yukinoshita's hand stopped, and she set her red pen down on the desk. Her shoulders slumped despondently. "I'm the one who should be sorry. I should have made sure to confirm your progress, and I should have known even you would make mistakes."

"Uh, naw, really, this was just me underestimating how long it would take. And wait, the heck? Is that super-high-level sarcasm...?" I asked.

She smiled and gave a little shake of her head. "Yes, but...I mean I was also underestimating the situation."

So she really was being sarcastic...

Regardless, it was clear that both of us had made errors in judgment. We had still not reached an understanding when it came to me, to her, or about ourselves. It was just like this moment of indeterminate day and night, when the colors of the twilight reached across the sky out the window, and by the time you think you've figured it out, the moment has passed, and the colors are changing again.

"I'm the one who's done the least," she muttered, looking vaguely out at the glow of the sunset.

"It's enough. Neither I nor Yuigahama are any good at keeping a schedule or project management. And Isshiki is decent at talking big and balancing the books, but she isn't the type who can keep a project moving systematically…," I answered as I gazed out at the same sunset.

But she and I probably saw different colors. Was hers red, pink, scarlet, crimson, burgundy? Or was it orange? I wouldn't really mind no matter what shade it was.

"Well, so…you've been fairly helpful." Pulling my eyes from the window, I returned my attention to the student council room.

The sunlight streaming in cast crimson over the room. When I turned to Yukinoshita, sitting beside me, her head was downcast, and I couldn't tell what was on her face. But her ears and neck, peeking out from under her hair, were also that same color.

"…I…hope so." That little murmur seemed lacking in confidence, almost sulking, after a short sigh.

But that was only for an instant. She immediately lifted her face, sweeping her hair off her shoulders to say in her usual commanding tone, "I'll make some adjustments on the back end to buy you time."

"Ah? O-okay… Wait, you can do that?" I asked, but she didn't answer.

Instead, she started dialing some number on her cell phone. "…Yuigahama? There's been a change of plans. If it's not completed on time, then send in the text that's done and submit, inserting dummy text for the final portion, and then we'll revise it in the proofread. That's all. Can you also tell that to Isshiki? …Yes, thank you." She hung up, then gave me a look that seemed to be confirming, *Were you listening?*

"…Is that okay?" I asked.

"This is ultimately only an emergency measure in the event we fail to make it in time. I have included the costs of the extra revisions in the budget, just in case, so there's no problem there. If that happens, I'm afraid of not being able to do the final proofread anymore…but there's no way around that, this time," Yukinoshita said with a smile.

She'd even planned out, as a last resort, a little grace period in the schedule, on the off chance something unexpected occurred.

Good grief, after all that ragging on me for being soft, who is it being soft this time?

Well, I can't deny that I am, in fact, soft myself. However, even if I'm easy on myself, the flexibility will sometimes make me snap back in the opposite direction. So her being so forgiving with me made me want to turn down her kindness.

Tossing back the remainder of my coffee, I slammed it down on the table. The clash of the steel can on the steel desk made a clang.

"I'll finish it," I declared, and I faced the computer once more.

"…All right. Then do your best," she said quietly and briefly, but it was enough to reach my ears.

× × ×

Maybe it was thanks to the break, or maybe it was thanks to the sugar content of the MAX Coffee reaching my brain, but my hands never stopped on the keys.

As I wrote on without looking at the clock, I never even noticed Yuigahama and Isshiki coming into the student council room. The three girls all sat down in a cluster at a diagonal from me, just staring at me without speaking, waiting anxiously for me to finish writing.

I-it's hard to write like this…

Nevertheless, I put one sentence after another, then finished it off with a line to tie it together at the end. I pressed the Enter key then, but my hands refused to leave the keyboard right away. I just ran my eyes over that one line countless times, making sure to myself that I had no more words in me, until my heart understood that finally, I had reached completion.

"*Now* I'm finally done…"

The strength left my body all at once, and I leaned into the back of the chair, letting my arms dangle.

When I heaved a sigh of relief, Yukinoshita came to the seat next to me. "Do you mind if I look?"

"…Sure." I pushed the laptop over to her, and she immediately began checking it.

Yuigahama and Isshiki watched with tense expressions. I, however, had not much tension at all. *Why? Because now I'm free! Deadline? What deadline?! Fwa-ha-ha! I'm free!* Suppressing the desire to shriek, I waited for her to finish reading.

And then, after some time passed, she looked up from the computer. "…No issues. Isshiki, your turn."

"R-roger!" Next, Isshiki began the final check. But if it had gone through Yukinoshita's approval, it was probably fine.

And with this, my work was done. Maaan, a world without deadlines is the best!

As the feeling of release filled my brain with a drunken haze, Yuigahama and Yukinoshita spoke to me.

"Hikki, thanks."

"…Nice work."

"Yeah, thanks, guys. Sorry it was late." Oh, good gracious, I was experiencing such a feeling of euphoria, I'd accidentally let myself believe I'd accomplished this on my own, but this time, if not for the others observing me, I would probably definitely have bailed before I'd finished.

When you take that into consideration, you might in fact say it was their presence monitoring me that was causing me to experience this current elation.

…So that means, in other words, that editors and deadlines are like a dangerous drug. They should absolutely be outlawed. Say no to deadlines.

"I've checked it. No problems," Isshiki said as she slammed the laptop shut.

Yukinoshita nodded back at her. "We've managed to make it in time, so how about I brew some tea for us in the clubroom?"

"Time for an after-party!" cheered Yuigahama.

"Yeah!" Isshiki replied with equal enthusiasm.

Yukinoshita shot Isshiki a cold glare. "You do one last check of the whole thing. And have Miss Hiratsuka skim over it as well. That's the editor-in-chief's job."

"Whaaat?" Isshiki whined. Yukinoshita's eyebrows twitched.

Picking up on that aura, Yuigahama cut between them. "Come on, we'll still be here, so you can just come over once you're done."

"*Wahhh…* All right, I'll nail this quick, then go right over." And before Isshiki had even finished saying the words, she squeezed her pen. Her eyes wide like saucers, she started checking over everything.

With that sight still in the corner of my eye, I went out into the hallway.

On the way to the clubroom, Yukinoshita let out a short sigh. "…If only she would have dredged up that sort of motivation from the start."

"She can do it if she tries, huh?" observed Yuigahama.

"Some people are like that. They can't do it unless they're under pressure," I said with a wry smile.

With a mean-spirited grin, Yukinoshita looked at me. "My, who could you be talking about?"

"It's just human nature."

× × ×

The Service Club room heater had been repaired the day before, so in a drastic change from the other day, it was warm and cozy.

It wasn't like the student council room was particularly uncomfortable, but I could relax better in the clubroom. It wasn't really an emotional thing—I feel like it was more instinctual, more territorial. Well, after frequenting an area for nearly a year, a dog or cat would treat it as their territory. I'm no different.

However, I did get the impression that due to the past few days of work editing the free magazine, this familiar space had become a little disorganized.

As Yukinoshita was making the tea, Yuigahama and I decided to clean up.

We gathered together all the papers and disposed of the garbage. After a while, we finished up, and I was sitting my exhausted body down. Yuigahama made this *ah* sound. Turning around, I saw her holding the camera I'd used for the interviews.

"Hey, let's take some pictures. Of the Service Club!" Yuigahama suggested, and a little wrinkle came together in Yukinoshita's forehead. Seeing her reaction, Yuigahama tilted her head like she was asking permission. Yukinoshita gave a little shake of her head in response, and this time, Yuigahama cocked her head in the other direction.

As the two of them were arguing back and forth with facial expressions, the door to the clubroom rattled open.

"I turned it in, quick and dirty!" Isshiki announced as she came in.

Uhhh, you didn't need to say the "quick and dirty" part...

When Isshiki noticed Yuigahama with the camera in hand, she sounded surprised. "Oh, so you guys had the student council camera? Are you still using it?"

"She says she's going to take a photo of the Service Club," Yukinoshita answered, as if she had nothing to do with this club.

You're a member, too, right...? Wait, you're the captain, right?

"Then I'll take it for you," said Isshiki.

"You be in the picture, too, Iroha-chan!"

"Yes, another time, definitely! ...So first, all the members of the

Service Club." Though Isshiki was smiling, she refused bluntly and just held out her hand. Maybe this was her way of being nice.

Yuigahama seemed to understand this, as she handed the camera right over. "Oh? Thanks. Then please do! Let's all take one together after!"

"Um, I haven't said anything about taking one yet, though…"

"You just don't know when to give up, Yukinon," Yuigahama said flatly, leaving Yukinoshita at a loss for words.

Well, Yukinoshita's obviously going to fold in the end anyway… She could try to resist, but the end result would be the same. I know the feeling.

But I remembered there was a problem with that camera. "…By the way, there's no more space on the memory card."

"Ohhh, yeah. 'Cause you took *sooo* many of the tennis club," teased Isshiki.

"What would you be taking pictures of, to use up that much space…?" Yukinoshita said with exasperation.

Yuigahama thought about it for a moment, then gave a big nod. "The tennis club… Sai-chan, huh…? I can see that."

"That makes sense to you, Yui?!" Isshiki wailed.

So she's finally given up, huh…? Wait, what if she's acknowledged us…?, I was thinking, when Isshiki clapped her hands, then rummaged around in the pocket of her blazer.

"If there's no space, *theeen* are you okay with this phone?" Isshiki asked as she pulled out my phone. That reminded me that I hadn't gotten it back from her that day.

"Ahhh, well, there's plenty of space, so it's fine," I said.

"Then I'll take it with this!" she suggested with a wink, raising the phone straightaway. Was this also her version of being nice? Frankly, when it comes to her, I have no clue…

"Ummm, then you can just sit down right there, and Yui and Yukinoshita can be, like, standing behind you."

"Okay!"

"U-um… Agh…"

Isshiki briskly gave directions, and Yuigahama took Yukinoshita's arm. It seemed Yukinoshita had finally given up resisting, and the both of them lined up behind me. …*Behind me?*

"…Huh? Isn't this arrangement kind of weird? Don't you think this kinda makes it look like a family portrait? Shouldn't we spread out a bit more?" *And, like, they're close! Too close! I know it's for a photo, but being so close makes me a little anxious, so please spare me.*

When I tried to scooch my chair away to get some distance, my shoulders were held down from both sides. Looking up, I saw an ice-cold smile on Yukinoshita's face.

"You don't know when to give up, Hikigaya."

"Says you…"

"We're good to go, Iroha-chan!" Yuigahama shoved at my shoulder, too, as she called out to Isshiki.

"Right, then here I go! Say cheese!" There was the sound of the shutter, along with the flash going off a bunch of times.

Agh, I'm definitely making a weird face… This is like a family portrait…

I was still angsting over the whole situation when Isshiki moseyed over and returned my phone. "Here… It's a good photo," she said, and she smiled in a bit of a grown-up way. I wasn't about to ask what she meant by that. I'm sure it was nothing more than exactly what she said.

"Send that to me, Hikki. Oh, but wait, Iroha-chan, let's take one together!"

"Okaaay! Then you take it for us, please." Isshiki gave my shoulder a pat, then hurried over to Yuigahama and Yukinoshita.

"I would rather not…," said Yukinoshita.

"Nope. Let's take it all together!" Yuigahama told her.

"So what order do we stand in?" Isshiki asked.

As the three of them quibbled over the composition, I took a quiet look at my phone. There was the photo we'd just taken of the Service Club.

...Yeah, it's not as bad as I thought. I mean, it's not very portrait-y.

And plus, it seemed to me that this photo depicted the way the Service Club was, the way we were, that I hadn't known how to write about then. So it really wasn't as bad as I'd thought.

I still had no idea what to call it, or how to define it. Maybe that was how we could share it. I'm sure of it, in fact. If you were to put it into words, it would probably give form to those conflicting feelings and tie them down.

"Hikki, take the picture!"

"...Right-o," I answered Yuigahama, and I stood up to point my phone camera at them.

Yuigahama, with her usual bright and cheerful smile.

Isshiki, with her first-class pose.

And then Yukinoshita, embraced by each of them from either side, looking a little annoyed, but also with shyly blushing cheeks.

How many more trivial, mundane scenes would we be able to accumulate?

One day, when I'm old enough to feel nostalgia for this image, what sort of pain will accompany that memory?

With these thoughts in mind, I snapped the photo.

And thus the night grows late at the **Hikigaya** household.

The cold wind of midwinter blasted against the windows, loudly rattling the glass in the living room. I pushed myself up from where I was sprawled in the *kotatsu* to get a look outside. The night had gotten quite late, and all that lay among the pitch-black were the scattered lights of streetlamps.

Our parents had told us they had some issues to deal with at work coming up to the end of the fiscal year, so they would be coming home at late o'clock. It was just me and Komachi in the house. I hadn't had the time to talk face-to-face with her lately, either. There wasn't much time left until the day of her tests. That night, as usual, she was cooped up in her room, doubtlessly studying hard for her entrance exams.

The cold wind was whooshing again. Though the heat was on low in the living room where I was, the cold air radiated from the window.

Oh, I wonder if Komachi feels cold…, I thought, looking over to the wall adjoining her room, but I couldn't hear any sounds from over there. It was late. She'd be asleep around now.

Guess I'll go to bed soon, too, I thought, but unable to resist the comfort of the *kotatsu*, I collapsed again and rolled over. I must have kicked the cat in the process, as there was some restless stirring, and then the family cat, Kamakura, crawled out. He shot me a grumpy look.

Oh, s-sorry…, I silently apologized.

Kamakura snorted, then started grooming himself with his tongue. Once he was done, his ears stuck straight up, and his face turned to the door.

Then there was a rattle as the door slid open, and Komachi, wearing my hand-me-down tracksuit, lumbered in.

"What's up. You're still awake?" I asked.

"I nodded off at a weird time, and now I'm super-awake…," she said, looking at me with her big round eyes.

Ahhh, I know that feeling. That thing where you come home and collapse on the sofa or in the *kotatsu*, and then you pass out, and then you can't sleep at night.

Sometimes those naps will be effective, but the time of year is what it is. The period before an exam will inevitably destroy your lifestyle rhythm.

"Even if you're not sleepy, go to bed," I told her. "Or you'll have a bad time tomorrow."

"Yeah. Komachi's hungry, so once I've eaten something." Komachi rotated her shoulders, then headed off into the kitchen.

Once there, she let out a tiny cry of distress. *What could it be?* I wondered, and when I wiggled out of the *kotatsu* to take a peek, she was gazing at the fridge vacantly.

…Ahhh, crap. That reminds me—Mom asked me to go shopping just a while ago. She'd called me on the phone so randomly, I'd wondered what the heck was going on. And then I'd been so busy with the production of the free magazine, I'd completely forgotten about shopping. And I'd just thrown together whatever for myself…so I got the feeling we didn't have much left in the way of ingredients. Komachi was moaning as she gazed at the empty fridge.

I'm sorry, Big Bro forgot to go shopping… Oh no, at this rate, Komachi will starve because of me!

"…I've got no choice. I'll make something for you," I said, tapping Komachi's shoulder.

But she turned around and shook her head. "Huh…? It's fine."

"Hey, no need to be polite."

"No, it really is fine. I mean, like, seriously don't, please. Komachi doesn't want to get sick," she rattled off quickly as she waved her hands aggressively.

She didn't even have the decency to play it off as a joke… But when I do cook, she does basically eat it. What a kind girl she is! But she should be careful how she talks!

"I'm kind of hungry, too. I'm cooking anyway. So it won't be out of my way, really." Prodding at her back, I went to stand at the kitchen counter.

Komachi nodded reluctantly. "Well, if you insist…," she said, but she seemed uneasy about what I would do, restlessly following me around as I fished through the cupboards and fridge, almost monitoring me.

I found eggs, milk and *chikuwa* in the fridge, then dug up some instant ramen and canned corned beef from the shelf. This'd be enough.

When I lined these ingredients up in a proud array on the counter, Komachi popped her face out from behind me. "If I eat something like *that* at this hour, Komachi'll get fat…"

"It's all right, it's all right! Any Komachi is cute."

"Eugh. You should think before you speak…"

While Komachi was busy grumbling, I filled a pot with water and set it on the stove. The trick here is to make the amount of water about 70 percent of what it normally would be. I started frying up the corned beef and the *chikuwa*.

Komachi came up to my side, closely examining each of these ingredients. "…Wait, Bro, you've been eating stuff besides this, right?"

"When Mom cooks, I eat normal food. Though I forgot to shop today, so, well, this is more or less what I made."

"There's no vegetables…"

"Dude cooking doesn't come with nutrition. The cow eats vegetables. It's fine."

"The cow probably eats nothing but grains… You're hopeless…" Komachi trailed off, and then she opened up a shelf, stretching as hard as she could to reach to the back. "We do have some seaweed. And then we could rehydrate this wakame… Guess I'll open a can of corn, too."

"Ohhh, that's pretty fancy…" I watched Komachi, impressed, as she briskly arranged some toppings, before I reached out to the carton of milk.

When Komachi noticed that, she grabbed my hand in a claw. Her expression was weirdly serious. "Bro, what are you doing with the milk? I don't know what you're thinking, but it's scaring me, so stop."

"You don't? This makes it pseudo-tonkotsu-style," I said, tipping the milk into the pot.

Instantly, Komachi shrieked. "I told you to stoppp!"

"What? Like, this is what makes it good."

Ignoring Komachi's sniffling, I finished off the meal without a hitch. I dropped in the eggs, let it boil for a bit, then split the ramen into bowls. I dumped the fried corned beef and *chikuwa* in. Then you top it with the seaweed and corn…and voilà!

Komachi was just standing there motionless with her brow knitted, so I pushed her along toward the *kotatsu*. Proudly setting down the two bowls before us, I handed her chopsticks and a ceramic spoon. "There."

Komachi timidly brought her chopsticks to her mouth. And then the tension in her cheeks softened. "…Oh. It's surprisingly good," she murmured, and after that, blowing on the noodles and soup to cool it, she slurped it up. Relieved by her surprisingly positive reaction, I started eating, too.

Since neither of us could take it too hot, we didn't eat that fast. As we leisurely and slowly enjoyed our meal, Komachi muttered as if she'd suddenly remembered, "Your cooking is just as bad as always… It brings me back." She was looking down at her bowl, a gentle smile on her lips.

Way back, when Komachi was in elementary school, on occasional days like this when our parents were late coming home, the two of us had cooked and eaten together. I'd only been able to do dude cooking like this back then, too, but despite that, Komachi had never complained… Wait, she had complained. A lot… But nevertheless, she'd eaten it. The memory was very nostalgic, and also embarrassing.

"Rude. It's way better than last time. I mean, there's been a lot of progress in instant ramen."

"True. And you haven't made any!" Komachi fired back, then snickered before she continued, "But you know, you should learn to make something a bit more legitimate."

"Well, that is an important skill for a househusband, huh?"

"Well, yeah, but I don't think that's ever gonna happen. I mean in university or when you get a job, you'll eventually leave home, right? Then you have to cook for yourself!"

"Uh, I don't plan to ever leave home…"

Komachi shot me a cold glare. "Get out."

"O-okay…" *Do you hate me?* I thought, examining her expression.

But she cleared her throat, sneaking her gaze away, and then with a blush on her cheeks, glancing up at me, she said in the most endearing tone, "Well, if you just can't cook no matter what, then Komachi wouldn't mind *veeery* occasionally putting on the wife hat and going to cook for you… Oh, that was worth a lot of points, in Komachi terms!"

"The assumption that you're kicking me out of the house scores low, though…"

Our conversation about meaningless things continued until our ramen dinner was finished.

"Thanks for the meal," Komachi said with a polite bow of her head, before letting out a sigh of satisfaction and plopping straight down on her side.

"Yeah, you're welcome. All right, then get back to your room and go to bed already," I said to her, since it seemed like she'd fall asleep right there in the *kotatsu*.

Komachi responded with vague groan but then gasped as if something had just occurred to her, jerking up into a sitting position. "I wanna eat something sweet!"

"There isn't anything." I couldn't offer her anything besides my sweet face, my sweet words, and my sweetly naive ideas.

Of course that wasn't enough for her, and Komachi hopped to her feet. "Then how about we go to the convenience store?"

"A girl shouldn't be going out alone at this hour."

"It's fine if I'm not alone, right?" She slid her hand toward mine.

... Well, I guess I'll be a proper big brother for once.

× × ×

The stars were beautiful that night. The wind was blowing hard, and the air was clear. The moon, stars, streetlamps, and the lines of lights from houses illuminated the nighttime streets.

Nobody was out and about but us, and Komachi's voice rang out into the quiet. "Yeeeks, it's freezing! Brr! It's so coooold!"

"Yeah, it really is cold..."

As the both of us were shivering at the sudden drop in temperature, Komachi smacked into my back. Then her hand slid around to take my arm. "...Yeah. It's warm like this, and it's also worth a lot of Komachi points," she declared, looking up at my face.

It was hard to walk and embarrassing like this, and I was getting sick of her attempts at point scoring, so I reached out to her head to peel her off.

But then Komachi murmured, "There's not much time until exams…and once that's over, it's graduation… Then a new school, huh?"

Her expression contained none of her earlier glee. She was just gazing with melancholy at the streetlights that dotted the dark night. Seeing the anxiety in her eyes, I stopped my efforts to peel her off.

"Komachi."

She looked up. "Hmm? What, Bro?"

I dropped my hand on her head, then scrubbed it around. "I'll be waiting at high school."

"…Uh-huh." Maybe it was just the weight of my hand, but Komachi's face turned down. But there was strength in her soft voice.

The city at night was so quiet it was scary. We couldn't be sure of the ground at our feet, and the wind was cuttingly cold. I couldn't know when this long winter night would turn to dawn, but the time was clearly moving onward. Though the sky above was dark, the spring constellations would come to twinkle there again.

The seasons change, as do the connections between people in endless flux. Would someone new come to that clubroom, too? Maybe so, maybe not. And then in less than a year, I would leave it.

If Winter comes, can Spring be far behind? Eventually, I will also have my final look at this night sky, too.

So then, for the moment, with the warmth at my side…

…I will look up at the starry sky and walk.

Afterword

Good evening, this is Wataru Watari.

How are all you readers spending this time, near winter's end, when the new season is coming? For me: work.

This is nothing new, but ever since I started working, around New Year's, so many things come at once, and it's quite miserable, and this time has been no exception. As usual, I am spending every day on nothing but work. I blame everything on the end of the fiscal year and editing. (Can you feel my indignation?)

However, perhaps it's this sort of flurry that makes life exciting, and each day the richer for it... Kidding! If you can start saying that, you basically pass as a corporate cog! Yay.

Speaking of the mundane, there is a tendency for that word to refer to days with truly nothing out of the ordinary, no ups and downs at all. But I think even without any big incidents or accidents, even just the repetition of similar days can be occupied with all sorts of feelings and dealing with many struggles. For example, even during the day in, day out of work, work, work, you'll be like *I'm gonna knock him out* or *I'm gonna sock her* or *I've already punched that one.* Such a fluctuation of emotions. Every day is a day as a corporate cog.

And during that *everyday life*, what did he think, how did she feel? What sort of expressions do they have as they remember those days and talk about them?

And so, on that note, this has been *My Youth Romantic Comedy Is Wrong, As I Expected*, Volume 10.5.

And below, the acknowledgments.

Holy Ponkan⑧: Irohasuuuu. With Iroha on the cover, it's been like, this volume has been all Irohasu! Irohasu 100 percent! It was the best! Thank you very much, Irohasu.

To my editor, the great Hoshino: *C'mon, I can get the next one on time, ga-ha-ha!* The Wataru Watari who has said that is dead. Gone. I'll do a proper job this time! I'm not lying this time! Thank you very much. *Ga-ha-ha!*

To everyone involved with the media franchise: As always, thank you very much for your help. I've continued to cause trouble with the TV anime and other things, and I'm very sorry. I hope you will continue to support me.

To all my readers: I'm very sorry for always making those of you looking forward to the new book wait. I'm making steady progress on the main story as well, so I would be happy if you would watch over me warmly for a while. I would be extremely glad if you would continue to support *My Youth Romantic Comedy Is Wrong, As I Expected* in the future as well, with the TV anime that's starting in April, the manga adaptation, and other media.

Now, I've used up my page count about here, so I'll lay down my pen. Next time, let's meet again in *My Youth Romantic Comedy Is Wrong, As I Expected*, Volume 11!

On a certain day in February, while drinking the nutritional tonic MAX Coffee, friend of all-nighters,

Wataru Watari

Translation
Notes

Chapter 1 ··· One of these days, we'll probably find a simple job even **Yoshiteru Zaimokuza** can handle.

P. 5   "I was only liable for Totsuka—down to the tiniest details. Call me 'Tiny Tots' for short. Everyone knew I was a hard-core Totsuka stan. If he had concerts, I'd bring a homemade fan with his name on it. You know, 'Tiny Tots' is kinda cute." The original Japanese gag here is on *Totsuka tantou* (in charge of Totsuka) abbreviated to *Totsuka-tan*, and then he says, "But when you write Totsuka-tan in hiragana, then it looks abnormally cute." *Tan* is a childish suffix, more diminutive than *chan*.

P. 7   "Someone get this guy a Happy Meal. Do they make a Slaphappy Meal…?" This whole section hinges on the fact that *medetai* in Japanese means both "happy" and "naive." So when he pulls out the English word *happy*, he's actually calling Zaimokuza naive.

P. 8   "In a world like ours, where you can't even have little dreams…" is a line from a song with a title that can be translated as "Poison: this world where you can't say what you want to say." It's famous for being the OP of the *Great Teacher Onizuka* live-action drama—*GTO* is basically a quirky inspirational teacher show.

P. 10 **"...send an e-mail to whoever's ranked at the top on Let's Do a Novelist..."** Zaimokuza says Shousetsuka wo Yarou, a blatant riff on Shousetsuka ni Narou (Let's be a novelist), a website for self-published fiction that has been the birthplace for many light-novel series, such as *Re:ZERO*, *Konosuba*, etc.

P. 10 **"...enough to give you nausea, heartburn, indigestion, upset stomach, diarrhea? Pepto-Bismol!"** In Japanese, they use an old ad slogan for famotidine, a drug discovered by Yamanouchi Pharmaceutical: "Stomachache? Heartburn? Yamanouchi!"

P. 10 **"'Tis true that it's difficult to get hired straight out of university. But changing jobs is another matter! When you're on my level, you can slip into an editing agency or smaller publisher and get hired at a better company after you have sufficient experience."** Traditionally speaking, full-time workers in Japan are hired straight out of university and employed for life. It's less common to take someone from another company, because it's believed you're used to one way of doing things, and you'll have difficulty blending in with the company culture.

P. 11 **"...I could get insta-hired at Gagaga Bunko, at least..."** Gagaga is the Japanese publisher of this series.

P. 11 **"Say what you will, Shogakukan was still one of the Big Three..."** The Big Three in Japanese publishing are Kodansha, Shueisha, and Shogakukan, with Kadokawa cutting in to make it four.

P. 11   **"A *true partner* who could see and hear the same things as I…"** This is a quote from *Tales of Zestiria* that was used as a tagline in a bunch of promotional material.

P. 11   **"*Isono, let's play ball!*"** is a line that Nakajima, the best friend, is always saying in the long-running anime *Sazae-san*.

P. 12   **"Things like *Shirakaba* and *Garakuta Bunko* were in textbooks."** *Shirakaba* and *Garakuta Bunko* were literary magazines in the early twentieth century and late nineteenth century, respectively.

P. 12, 13   **"…or even on how to win a game of rock-paper-scissors that followed a Sunday anime."** The anime *Sazae-san* started the trend of the title character engaging in a game of rock-paper-scissors with the audience after the next episode preview.

P. 13   **"*Did you know, Raiden?*"** is a line that comes up repeatedly in the 1980s martial arts manga *Sakigake!! Otokojuku* (Charge, boys' school), whenever the bystanders needed to explain things happening in a fight. It was one of the earliest manga that did that a lot and was a bit of a trope-setter.

P. 16   **"Isn't that, like, a brand of gummy bears?"** The original Japanese gag here was on the slang term *chiiremu*, which comes from "cheater harem," which does not mean infidelity, but rather an overpowered hero with a harem. Isshiki assumes it's related to Chiitara, a brand of 7-Eleven cheese snacks.

P. 17   **"*I can see right through you!*"** *Sukesuke daze!* is the catchphrase of Keigo Atobe in *Prince of Tennis*.

P. 18   **"These '16 No-Nos'..."** "Nai Nai 16" is the name of a song by the 1980s boyband Shibugaki-tai. The "16" here probably refers to sixteen years old, and the lyrics are about not having love and whatnot.

P. 18   **"Enduring the heat and cold in the summer and the winter..."** Comiket is held twice a year, once in summer and once in winter, and the lineup to get into the building can be very long.

P. 25   **"About the only people with this much energy have got to be the Kinki Kids, or Yoshida Terumi."** "Kinki no Yaruki Manman Songu" (Kinki's super enthusiastic song) is the name of an OP for the *Chibi Maruko-chan* anime by the Kinki Kids. *Yoshida Terumi no Yaruki MANMAN!* (Yoshida Terumi's super enthusiasm) was a long-running radio show.

P. 26   **"You're talking about *SPA!*..."** *SPA!* magazine is a men's weekly entertainment magazine with articles ranging from sex tips to financial advice.

P. 29   **"...that's practically like Seele. That's beyond impact; that's Second Impact."** As any good *otaku* should know, this is an *Evangelion* reference.

P. 31   **"Zaimokuza emphatically agreed with a dramatic flutter of his coat like William Smith Clark..."** William Smith Clark was an American professor whom the Japanese government hired as a foreign advisor in the Meiji period, and there's a famous statue of him in Hokkaido, which is most certainly what this line is referencing.

P. 34   *"Gotcha—which is short for I've <u>got</u> no idea what you're <u>chattering</u> on about."* The Japanese here is dropping some manga slang, *saparan*, short for "I have no idea what you're talking about."

P. 36   *"Talk about a winner..."* This particular wording, *kachigumi yan ke...*, is a quote from the fairies in *Humanity Has Declined*.

P. 40   **"Don-Don-Donuts, let's go nuts!"** This is what the girls in *Shirobako* swear around a box of donuts when they commit to making an anime. It's an anime about the anime industry.

Chapter 2 ⋯ Surely, **Iroha Isshiki** is made of sugar and spice and everything nice.

P. 49   *"I don't know everything. I just know what I know"* is a quote from Tsubasa Hanekawa of the *Monogatari* series.

P. 59   **"And then she gave me the kind of bold grin that made me feel uncomfortable... Guess there's two sweaters here now!"** In Japanese he said, "And then she grinned boldly... 'Cause sweater, get it?" He's making a pun between *nitto* (grin) and *nitto* (knit sweater).

P. 64   *"That's some really blatant Toki Soba there."* Toki Soba is a traditional *rakugo* narrative (a comic anecdote) that uses that same trick of number distraction. Basically, this is a trick that's literally hundreds of years old.

P. 64   *"You still have a long way to go!"* This particular expression is the catchphrase of Ryoma Echizen, protagonist of *Prince of Tennis*, which he says when he beats his opponents.

P. 68   **"If we're just talking mental fortitude, she's stronger than the Japan National rugby team..."** This is a reference to the mental coach Kaori Araki, who trained the Japan National team. She wrote a book about it called *The Way of Mental Training That Changed Japan National Rugby*.

P. 70   "Miss Hiratsuka would be ready and willing to have Naritake, if it would only nari-take her." The Japanese gag here is fairly nonsensical. It says Miss H is enthusiastic (*norinori*) about eating at Naritake, and she'd even be *narinari taketake* about it. This means nothing; it just plays off some other terms for excitement that are based off sound effects.

P. 82   *"What the heck? Who does she think she is? Princess Kaguya?"* "Princess Kaguya," or "The Tale of the Bamboo Cutter," is a classic folktale. Princess Kaguya has a bunch of suitors, and she makes impossible requests of them for her hand in marriage.

Chapter 3 ⋯ There lies **the deadline** they absolutely cannot fail to make.

P. 94   "What was it, 'People are nice'? *Places to hang ooout and good fooood and cute cafés are waiting*, right? The only part that fits is the food, huh? Guess I'm wrong." Hachiman is wildly misremembering a song from the children's anime *Manga Nihon Mukashibanashi* that goes, "Good snacks and warm food are waiting for the children's return."

P. 94   *"I can just see her imagining cake… It's not a Swiss roll."* The Japanese gag here is on *keihi* (funds) and *keihi* (cinnamon bark), and Hachiman says, "With your intonation, that's completely Chinese medicine."

P. 115   "I was totally raring to go, like, *Leave the camera work to me, snap-snap-snap…*" This is a reference to an Internet meme with ASCII cats that go, "Leave the paying to me! *Riprip* [the sound of a wallet opening]." *Baribari* can also mean "working hard."

P. 115   "As I nodded, I also went *Capisce!* with a sideways ☆ peace sign to acknowledge…" This is the catchphrase of Laala Manaka from the *Pretty Rhythm* spin-off anime *PriPara*.

P. 136 "There's a thing called temper for steel and men…" is a line from Kunihiko Kimishima in *s-CRY-ed*, the impactful one-liner shortly before his death.

P. 137 "…if I could make it now, then the laws of the universe meant nothing!" This is a quote from Exdeath, the final boss of *Final Fantasy V*. It's become a minor Internet meme, referenced whenever it seems like something incredible or disturbing might happen.